PENGUIN

P9-DVG-741

VENUS IN FURS

LEOPOLD VON SACHER-MASOCH was born in 1836 in Lemberg
(today Lvov), in the province of Habsburg Galicia. His father
was the police prefect of the city, and the family moved, within
the Habsburg monarchy, to Prague in 1848 and to Graz in 1854.
Sacher-Masoch attended the university in Graz, and though he
had previously grown up in urban environments where Ukrainian, Polish, and Czech were spoken, his education made him a
German writer. His earliest works were Habsburg histories,
about the monarchy in the sixteenth century, during the reign of
Charles V. In 1864 he wrote a novella, *Don Juan von Kolomea*,
set in Habsburg Galicia, and in 1865 a historical novel about
the eighteenth-century Habsburg chancellor Prince Kaunitz. In
1870 he published several novellas, conceived as part of a larger
fictional work, *The Testament of Cain*; one of these was *Venus
in Furs*, which earned him immediate notoriety for its unprece-
dented treatment of a man who passionately made himself the
slave of the woman he loved. Later works of fiction included
tales of the Viennese court, tales of the Russian court, Galician
tales, and Jewish tales. His literary fascination with Jewish scenarios, especially in Galicia, led to the public misconception that
he was himself Jewish. In 1872 he met Aurora Rümelin, who
married him and assumed the name, as well as the erotic per-
sona, of Wanda, the heroine of *Venus in Furs*. They had several
children together, and an unusual married life—which she later
recounted in her memoirs—focused on the fulfillment of his un-
conventional romantic obsessions. Sacher-Masoch emigrated
from the Habsburg monarchy in 1881, having been sentenced to
eight days in prison after a legal dispute with a publisher. Thereafter he lived in Germany, though he was unsympathetic to the
spirit of imperial German nationalism, and perhaps received better appreciation from the literary public in France, where he was
awarded the cross of the Legion of Honor in 1883. In 1890
Richard von Krafft-Ebing introduced "masochism" as a clinical
category in his *Psychopathia Sexualis*. When Sacher-Masoch died
in 1895, his works of fiction, and especially *Venus in Furs*, were
already widely recognized as giving literary expression to a not
uncommon, but previously little discussed, complex of romantic
and sexual fantasies.

LARRY WOLFF is professor of European history at Boston College. He is the author of *The Vatican and Poland in the Age of the Partitions*, of *Postcards from the End of the World: Child Abuse in Freud's Vienna*, of *Inventing Eastern Europe: The Map of Civilization on the Mind of the Enlightenment*, and of a forthcoming book, *Venice and the Slavs*.

JOACHIM NEUGROSCHEL has translated numerous books from French, German, Italian, Russian, and Yiddish. He has won three PEN translation awards and the French-American translation prize. He has also translated Thomas Mann, Hermann Hesse, and Alexandre Dumas for Penguin Classics.

LEOPOLD VON SACHER-MASOCH

Venus in Furs

Translated by
JOACHIM NEUGROSCHEL

With an Introduction by
LARRY WOLFF

and Notes by
JOACHIM NEUGROSCHEL

PENGUIN BOOKS

PENGUIN BOOKS
Published by the Penguin Group
Penguin Group (USA) Inc., 375 Hudson Street, New York, New York 10014, U.S.A.
Penguin Group (Canada), 90 Eglinton Avenue East, Suite 700, Toronto, Ontario,
Canada M4P 2Y3 (a division of Pearson Penguin Canada Inc.)
Penguin Books Ltd, 80 Strand, London WC2R 0RL, England
Penguin Ireland, 25 St Stephen's Green, Dublin 2, Ireland (a division of Penguin Books Ltd)
Penguin Group (Australia), 250 Camberwell Road, Camberwell, Victoria 3124,
Australia (a division of Pearson Australia Group Pty Ltd)
Penguin Books India Pvt Ltd, 11 Community Centre, Panchsheel Park,
New Delhi – 110 017, India
Penguin Group (NZ), 67 Apollo Drive, Rosedale, North Shore 0632, New Zealand
(a division of Pearson New Zealand Ltd)
Penguin Books (South Africa) (Pty) Ltd, 24 Sturdee Avenue, Rosebank,
Johannesburg 2196, South Africa

Penguin Books Ltd, Registered Offices: 80 Strand, London WC2R 0RL, England

This translation first published in Penguin Books 2000

LIBRARY OF CONGRESS CATALOGING-IN-PUBLICATION DATA
Sacher-Masoch, Leopold, Ritter von, 1835–1895.
[Venus im Pelz. English]
Venus in furs / Leopold von Sacher-Masoch ; translated from
the German by Joachim Neugroschel ; with an introduction by
Larry Wolff and notes by Joachim Neugroschel.
p. cm.
Includes bibliographical references.
ISBN 978-0-14-044781-1
1. Neugroschel, Joachim.   II. Wolff, Larry.   III. Title.

PT2461.S3V3513   2000
833'.8—dc21   99-055346

Printed in the United States of America
Set in Stempel Garamond

CONTENTS

v

INTRODUCTION

"MY MOST CHERISHED FANTASY"

"I feel justified in calling this sexual anomaly 'Masochism,' "
wrote Richard von Krafft-Ebing, creating a new clinical category
for his *Psychopathia Sexualis*, "because the author Sacher-
Masoch frequently made this perversion, which up to his time
was quite unknown to the scientific world as such, the substra-
tum of his writings." Krafft-Ebing, who introduced the term in
1890, was not merely borrowing the name of Leopold von
Sacher-Masoch as a convenient label; rather, the case histories in
the many editions of *Psychopathia Sexualis* indicated that Sacher-
Masoch, through his published writings and even through personal contacts, had already long exercised a sort of cult appeal
upon people who recognized their own sexual inclinations in his
literary work. Case 114 from the 8th edition of 1893 described a
man who longed to be "the slave of the beloved, referring for this
purpose to Sacher-Masoch's *Venus in Furs*." Case 57 from the
12th edition of 1903 told of a man who first began to fantasize
about slavery and flagellation when he read *Uncle Tom's Cabin*
as a boy; later he wondered whether he could hope to find
"sadistically constituted women like Sacher-Masoch's heroines,"
and whether it would be possible to find sexual satisfaction, "if
there were such women, and I had the fortune (!) to find one."
Case 68 told of a young artist who was most sexually aroused
when faced with female anger, and who "thought that only a
woman like the heroines of Sacher-Masoch's romances could
charm him." Case 80 described a man with a special interest in
licking women's feet, who actually corresponded with Sacher-
Masoch, and received guidance from the master:

One of these letters, dated 1888, shows as a heading the picture of a luxuriant woman, with imperial bearing, only half covered with furs and holding a riding-whip as if ready to strike. Sacher-Masoch contends that "the passion to play the slave" is widespread, especially among the Germans and Russians. In this letter, the history of a noble Russian is related who loved to be tied and whipped by several beautiful women. One day he found his ideal in a pretty young French woman and took her to his home.[1]

Sacher-Masoch was clearly ready to respond to his fans and appear as the leader of the masochistic movement with specially designed stationery to show his stripes. Rather like Krafft-Ebing, Sacher-Masoch also seemed to collect cases to demonstrate that his inclinations were widespread, no individual eccentricity but a common complex. Finally, in response to a select public of men who wondered whether they too might be fortunate enough to find women with whips who resembled his literary heroines, Sacher-Masoch affirmed the existence of the female "ideal," like the pretty young French woman ready to be taken home. This was the ideal that he himself had most vividly depicted for the reading public in his masochistic masterpiece, *Venus in Furs*.

"You've aroused my most cherished fantasy," says Severin, the hero of the novel, and he specifies the fundamental features of the fantasy:

> "*To be the slave of a woman, a beautiful woman, whom I love, whom I worship—!*"
> "And who mistreats you for it," Wanda broke in, laughing.
> "Yes, who ties me up and whips me, who kicks me when she belongs to another man."
> "And who, after driving you insane with jealousy and forcing you to face your successful rival, goes so far in her exuberance that she turns you over to him and abandons you to his brutality. Why not? Do you like the final tableau any less?"
> I gave Wanda a terrified look. "You're exceeding my dreams."
> "Yes, we women are inventive," she said. "Be careful. When you find your ideal, she might easily treat you more cruelly than you like."

"I'm afraid I've already found my ideal!" I cried and pressed
my hot face into her lap.[2]

Venus in Furs presents a protagonist in single-minded pursuit of
the realization of his fantasies, and the sympathetically perverse
part of the public responded precisely to those fantasies and the
fictional delineation of an ideal partner. Published in 1870, *Venus
in Furs* promptly attracted to Sacher-Masoch not only some gen-
eral notoriety but also the most important fan letter of his life. Aurora Rümelin, a young woman in Graz, where Sacher-Masoch
then lived, read the novel and wrote to him, composing the letter
together with an older female friend. "She sat down and wrote a
letter so shameless I did not believe she would actually mail it—
much less receive a response," recalled Rümelin, but Sacher-
Masoch replied immediately, reporting that he had read the letter
"with rapture."[3] The letter to Sacher-Masoch had been signed
"Wanda von Dunajew," the name of the heartless heroine of *Venus
in Furs*, and Aurora Rümelin, who eventually met and married
Sacher-Masoch, adopted the name as her own and tried to live up
to the ideal it expressed. Her memoirs, published as the *Confessions* of Wanda von Sacher-Masoch, after his death, constituted a
sort of astonishing housewife's lament, a harried account of trying
to raise the children and make ends meet, while keeping in mind
that at the end of a long day she still had to put on her furs, pick
up her whips, and become her husband's merciless ideal.

Sacher-Masoch's initial rapture at receiving a letter from
"Wanda von Dunajew" was intensified by his conviction that the
correspondent was a Russian princess. For the furred figure of
Wanda in *Venus in Furs*, the personification of voluptuous cruelty, was a specifically Slavic fantasy. Among the notoriously
powerful women whose names are invoked in the novel, from
Messalina and Delilah to Manon Lescaut and Madame Pompadour, none is mentioned more frequently or emphatically than
Catherine the Great. When Wanda would appear, "in her white
satin robe and in her red, ermine-trimmed kazabaika," with
powdered hair and a diamond tiara, Severin found that "she re-

minded me intensely of Catherine the Great."[4] Catherine was a figure of great interest to Sacher-Masoch, who put her into his fiction in the *Tales of the Russian Court*, published soon after *Venus in Furs*. For instance, at the beginning of the novella *Diderot in St. Petersburg*, Catherine is bored, and idly wishes there could be some conspiracy against her so that she could punish the rebels with the whip and decapitate the leaders; eventually, though without her knowing, the philosopher Diderot is sewn into a monkey's skin, mistaken for a great ape, and trained by the whip to perform entertaining tricks at the Russian court. It was, of course, the absolute power of the Russian tsarina that seemed so fascinating to Sacher-Masoch, just as in the eighteenth century she attracted the literary interest of the Marquis de Sade, who made her the mistress of the orgy, whip in hand, in the *History of Juliette*.

In *Venus in Furs* Wanda's costumes, with their fur trimmings and accessories, repeatedly bring Catherine to mind in the rapturous enthusiasm of Severin:

> A new, fantastic attire: Russian ankle-boots of violet, ermine-trimmed velvet; a gown of the same material, decorated with narrow stripes and gathered up with cockades of the identical fur; a short, close-fitting paletot similarly lined and padded with ermine; a high ermine cap à la Catherine the Great . . .[5]

Fantasies of Catherine, of Russia, and more generally of Eastern Europe thus appear as the crucial fur lining to the fundamental fantasies of slavery, flagellation, and abasement. One day Wanda takes Severin shopping in the local bazaar:

> There she looked at whips, long whips with short handles, the kind used on dogs.
> "These should do the job," said the vendor.
> "No, they're much too small," replied Wanda, casting a side-long glance at me. "I need a big—"
> "For a bulldog no doubt?" asked the merchant.
> "Yes," she cried, "the sort of whip that was used on rebellious slaves in Russia."[6]

Thus Sacher-Masoch manipulated the instruments and images of
Russian barbarism to enhance his fantasies of romantic cruelty
and sexual slavery. This aspect of his work was readily apparent
to contemporary reviewers, and *Venus in Furs*, upon its publica-
tion in 1870, was denounced accordingly in the *Neue Freie
Presse*, the great German liberal newspaper of Vienna. Sacher-
Masoch was censured as a dangerous artistic agent of "communism" and Russian nihilism.

> Whoever loves liberty and his country must fight with all his
> force against every attempt to import into Germany these nihilis-
> tic views. . . . If he [Sacher-Masoch] continues to play the nihilist,
> I would advise him not only to think in Russian but also to write
> in Russian, for in Germany there will be as little place for him and
> his works as for Russian barbarism, in the name of which his
> Wanda von Dunajew whips her lovers.[7]

Indeed, Sacher-Masoch did make use of Russian details and,
even more, played upon contemporary fears and fantasies about
Russia, in order to introduce an explosive deviation from the
conventional romantic forms of bourgeois Victorian society in
nineteenth-century Europe. Yet Sacher-Masoch insisted that his
own predilections were widespread among Germans as well as
Russians. One of Krafft-Ebing's informants, around the turn of
the century, reported on the presumed prevalence of such perversion, citing "the fact that every experienced prostitute keeps
some suitable instrument (usually a whip) for flagellation," and
noting that "all prostitutes agree that there are many men who
like to play 'slave'—i.e., like to be so called, and have themselves
scolded and trod upon and beaten." The conclusion was alarm-
ing: "The number of masochists is larger than has yet been
dreamed."[8] Evidently, the reviewer of *Venus in Furs*, who denounced the novella in 1870 for its insidious communism and nihilism, already had some inkling that the specter haunting
Europe might be the specter of masochism.

"THE MAGNIFICENT NATURE OF THE CARPATHIANS"

Sacher-Masoch was born in 1836 in the Galician city of Lemberg, today Lviv in Ukraine, and very near the nineteenth-century border between the Habsburg and the Russian empires. Under the Polish name of Lwów it had belonged to the Polish-Lithuanian Commonwealth, until annexed in 1772 by Austria in the first partition of Poland; the city then became the administrative center of the Habsburg province of Galicia. Sacher-Masoch was the son of a Habsburg police official of German Bohemian descent, who conserved law and order in Lemberg on behalf of the Metternich administration in Vienna. At that time the city, numbering around 50,000 inhabitants, was still predominantly Polish in population, though in addition to Austrian imperial officials, there were also increasingly important urban minorities, the Jews as well as the Ruthenians or Ukrainians, for whom the town was just becoming a center of emerging national culture. The 1830s was precisely the period when a small circle of young priests in the Uniate or Greek Catholic seminary in Lemberg began to urge the literary importance of the Ukrainian language. Habsburg officials, like Sacher-Masoch's father, were prepared to give limited encouragement to Ukrainian nationalism as a counterbalance to the conspiratorial national engagement of the Poles, who aspired to the restoration of an independent Poland, including Galicia.

Sacher-Masoch himself, though he lived in Galicia only until the age of twelve, maintained a lifelong fascination and sympathy with the peoples of the province, especially the Jews and the Ruthenians. He was particularly intrigued by the Hassidic movement, which was exceptionally important among Jews in Galicia, and he wrote about them with such philo-Semitic sympathy in his Jewish tales that he was widely suspected of being a Jew himself, as well as a nihilist and a communist. He described the women at the court of a Hassidic leader, the Zaddik of Sadogora, and could not resist focusing fetishistically on their furs:

The Zaddik's wife and daughters-in-law, his daughters and his nieces, were assembled. I felt as if I had been transported into the harem of the Sultan in Constantinople. All these women were beautiful, or at least pretty; both astonished and amused, they all looked at us with their big black-velvet eyes; they were all dressed in silk morning-gowns and long caftans made of silk or velvet and trimmed and lined with expensive furs. One could see all colors and kinds of furs: yellow and pink silk, green, red, and blue velvet, squirrel, ermine, marten, and sable.[9]

It would be all too easy to imagine how Sacher-Masoch might have invested this scene with his characteristic romantic fantasies, envisioning a rabbinical harem for masochistic Hassids, but in the tale itself he restrained his literary instincts and impulses. In *Venus in Furs* the Jews of Galicia appear in strictly secondary roles, never in furs; it is a Jewish dealer who sells Severin a photograph of Titian's *Venus with Mirror*, and another who sells him secondhand books, apparently including the memoirs of Casanova. When Severin leaves Galicia in a third-class railway compartment, playing the part of Wanda's servant, he must suffer the smell of onions in the company of Polish peasants and Jewish peddlers. Sacher-Masoch gives free rein to his fantasies in *Venus in Furs*, but his literary representation of Galicia is ethnographically precise.

Though he emphatically denied being a Jew, Sacher-Masoch proudly claimed to be of noble Ruthenian descent, on his mother's Masoch side of the family. This may or may not have been true, for his Masoch grandfather was born in the Habsburg Banat of Temesvar, part of modern Romania, and may himself have been of Czech or Slovak descent. Sacher-Masoch's national identity, however, like his sexual identity, was very much conditioned by his imagination, and so he imagined his Masoch ancestors to be Ruthenians, as he also liked to suppose that the Sacher family came originally from Habsburg Spain. "The name Sacher which people have so often taken for a Jewish name, is in reality of Oriental origin," he noted, insisting on an exotic descent from Spanish Moors. "People have already taken me for almost everything," he wrote, "for a Jew, a Hungarian, a Bohemian, and even for a woman."[10] A confused and complex identity was by no means unusual in a family whose ultimate allegiance lay with the Habsburg dynasty in a multinational empire. Sacher-Masoch himself was always patriotically committed to the Habsburgs, and explored the history of the dynasty in his works, ranging from the reign of Charles V to that of Maria Theresa. In 1880 Sacher-Masoch, so punctilious in his bizarre contracts of sexual slavery, was fighting with his publisher over business contracts, and the author was condemned to eight days in prison. He sent his wife, Wanda, to plead for him face-to-face with the Emperor Franz Joseph in Vienna, who declined to cancel the sentence. The following year Sacher-Masoch, in spite of his private enthusiasm for being bound, beaten, and abased, went into exile in Germany rather than go to prison in the Habsburg monarchy.

Sacher-Masoch's identity as a Slavic Ruthenian came not only from supposed descent, but also from an intense connection to the Galician village girl who became his wet nurse in his infancy:

> With her milk I sucked in the love of the Russian people, of my province, of my homeland. . . . Through my nurse Russian became the first language that I commanded, though in my parents' house Polish, German, and French were primarily spoken. And it was she who told me the wondrously beautiful Russian fairy tales, or sang, while rocking me, those Little Russian folk songs that stamped themselves upon my existence, my emotional world, and also all my later works.[11]

Thus he considered himself a Slav by origin, without actually distinguishing clearly between Ruthenian and Little Russian on the one hand, which would denominate modern Ukrainian, and Russian on the other hand, which would certainly have been alien to the province of Galicia and his Habsburg homeland. By the same token, the presumptively "Russian" identity of Wanda von Dunajew in *Venus in Furs* should perhaps be considered more generally suggestive of the Slavs of Eastern Europe. After all, even Catherine the Great, whom Wanda thrillingly resembled, was not actually Russian by birth, but a German princess who adopted a Russian identity.

Sacher-Masoch, though he was to make his career as a writer in German, did not actually begin his proper German education until his father was transferred to Prague in 1848; the young man eventually completed his studies at the university in Graz. Prague was a Czech and German city in the nineteenth century, and Graz, in Austrian Styria, was very close to Habsburg Slovenia. In short, the mingling of German and Slavic populations in the Habsburg monarchy in the nineteenth century was such that Sacher-Masoch could plausibly subscribe to a confusion of German and Slavic identities. *Venus in Furs*, though written in German, presented the Galician flagellant Severin von Kusiemski, also unspecifically Slavic, as a familiar figure from the author's native province. In the 1860s Sacher-Masoch had corresponded with the Ruthenian political leader Mykhail Kuzemsky.

In *Venus in Furs* Severin is identified as "a Galician nobleman and landowner," and his possession of estates makes it more likely that he would be Polish than Ruthenian, for, generally, the Poles of Galicia were the noble landowners, while the Ruthenians tended to be peasants working the land. Wanda is introduced as "a widow from Lwów," and Severin meets her at a resort in the Carpathian mountains, near the border between the Habsburg and the Russian empires. Excited at the possibility of becoming Wanda's slave, Severin walks in the mountains: "hoping to numb my passion, my yearning in the magnificent nature of the Carpathians."[12] The fantasies of Sacher-Masoch in *Venus in Furs* were conditioned by the ethnography and the geography of Habsburg Galicia, and that setting recurs not only in the Jewish tales, but also in a collection of specifically Galician tales. Another novella told the tale of *Don Juan von Kolomea*, today Kolomyia in Ukraine. Sacher-Masoch was very much a writer of his Habsburg homeland, but his was not the metropolitan literary landscape of Vienna; rather he defined his perspective from the remote and mountainous margins of the monarchy, where his literary fantasy played all the more freely. This same Galician terrain was revisited much later in the final fictional monument to the Habsburg monarchy, *Radetzky March*, by Joseph Roth, who was born in Galicia, not far from Lemberg, in the year before Sacher-Masoch's death.

In *Venus in Furs* Sacher-Masoch sets up an opposition between the northern land of Galicia and the southern Mediterranean domain of Venus. On the opening page of the novella, the marble statue Venus appears in a dream, comically sneezing from the cold of the northern climate: "The sublime being had wrapped her marble body in a huge fur and, shivering, had curled up like a cat." Later Severin explains that coldness is not only meteorological but also a moral and metaphorical matter, inasmuch as pagan Venus requires a fur to warm her in "the icy Christian world" of the north.[13] When Wanda and Severin leave Galicia together, they head for the south, to discover the pagan heritage and classical climate of Italy, though she nevertheless must pack up all her northern furs to travel, and he must carry them as her servant. Poland and Russia, up until the eighteenth century, always figured in European geography as lands of the north; thereafter, they began to be reclassified according to the cultural cartography of the Enlightenment, and came to be viewed together in accordance with the emerging modern idea of Eastern Europe. A distinction began to be made between Western Europe and Eastern Europe, the latter perceived as the more exotic and less civilized part of the continent. Furthermore, Eastern Europe was conceived as a domain of slavery, because of the supposed despotism of government, whether in the Russian or Ottoman empires, and also on account of the harsh conditions of serfdom, whether on the Polish or Russian estates. The disapproval that developed in Western Europe sometimes produced the opinion that in Eastern Europe people actually preferred to live in servitude, and when the Marquis de Custine published his celebrated account of traveling in Russia in 1839, he did not hesitate to pronounce the Russians to be "drunk with slavery."[14] Such perspectives must have conditioned the reception of *Venus in Furs* by nineteenth-century readers, who would have interpreted Severin's ecstatic sexual slavery in the context of his origin in Galicia. Sacher-Masoch's first biographer, Carl Felix von Schlichtegroll, writing in 1901, described Galicia as "melancholy, strange, half-wild, half-overcultivated." The most recent biographer, Bernard Michel, writing in 1989, argues that Galician scenarios were essential to Sacher-Masoch, because, when set "in a remote land, considered exotic and therefore backward," the author's extraordinary fantasies "became conceivable" to the public.[15] Thus, Sacher-Masoch, writing in German, was offering his readers a scenario of Slavic exoticism, which could be received in the context of contemporary prejudices concerning the barbarism of Eastern Europe. Sacher-Masoch himself was susceptible to the exoticism of his own native Galicia, as indicated by the imaginative maneuver that made the Hassidic ladies of Sadogora appear as a sort of Turkish harem.

In considering Severin's eagerness to become a slave, one must keep in mind that there was indeed actual slavery in the world during Sacher-Masoch's lifetime. When *Venus in Furs* was published in 1870, black slaves in the United States had only recently been freed by the Emancipation Proclamation of 1863 and the Thirteenth Amendment of 1865, while the serfs of Russia had been liberated from their conditions of bondage in 1861. In the Habsburg monarchy itself, including Galicia, serfdom had not been fully abolished until 1848. The novella is imbued with a perverse nostalgia for slavery, and Wanda becomes "melancholy" at the thought that "slavery doesn't exist in our country." Severin replies: "Then let's go to a country where it still exists, to the Orient, to Turkey." Wanda soon reconsiders, and proposes that they go to Italy instead: "What good is having a slave where everyone has slaves? I want to be *alone in having a slave*." Once settled in Florence, she turns out to have not only a Slavic slave in Severin, but, mysteriously, others as well: "Three young, slender African women came in—carved out of ebony, as it were, and clad entirely in red satin. Each woman was clutching a rope." At Wanda's command, they bind Severin in preparation for a whipping, and then vanish suddenly "as if the earth had swallowed them up." Their nearly supernatural entrance and exit suggest the freedom of fantasy with which Sacher-Masoch develops the theme and variations of slavery. Severin's contract with Wanda specifies, "Not only may Frau von Dunajew punish her slave as she sees fit for the slightest oversight or offense, but she also has the right to mistreat him at whim or merely as a pastime, however it happens to please her, and she even has the right to kill him if she so wishes. In short: he is her absolute property."[16] His legal subjection to her, however extraordinary as an act of enthusiastic self-annihilation, stipulated conditions that were not altogether alien to European and American society up until the middle of the nineteenth century.

When Sacher-Masoch was ten years old, in 1846, Galicia experienced an episode of social conflict of such traumatic intensity that it haunted the Polish national consciousness for the rest of the century, and also left a powerful impression on the son of the Lemberg police prefect. The outbreak of a Polish national insurrection in the free city of Cracow sparked conspiratorial activity in Galicia, and the Habsburg attempts to preserve their authority in the province involved countenancing, if not actually encouraging, a jacquerie that led to the ferocious massacre of the insurrectionary noble landowners. Thus the peasants of Galicia served the purposes of Habsburg rule, proving that their hatred of the local landowners far outweighed any sense of Polish national solidarity. The principal peasant leader, Jakub Szela, infamous in Polish national memory, was politely received in the Sacher-Masoch home in Lemberg after the massacre, and became a lifelong figure of fascination for the author. Thus, from childhood, Sacher-Masoch had to confront the violent social tensions that invested the circumstances of Habsburg loyalty in Galicia, and in 1846 he received a glimpse of what it might mean to overturn temporarily the relations between nobles and peasants, the powerful and the powerless. The actual class tensions of the nineteenth century conditioned the fantastic inversions by which a nobleman like Severin von Kusiemski, or Leopold von Sacher-Masoch, played with the possibility of absolute subjection.

"YOU'VE CORRUPTED MY IMAGINATION"

"During recent years facts have been advanced which prove that Sacher-Masoch was not only the poet of Masochism, but that he himself was afflicted with this anomaly," observed Krafft-Ebing in the 12th edition of *Psychopathia Sexualis*. Indeed, after Sacher-Masoch's death in 1895, there followed several revealing publications concerning his life, including that of Schlichtegroll in 1901, which made use of material from the author's private diary that has since been lost. Wanda published her *Confessions* in 1906, still angry at having been abandoned by Sacher-Masoch for a different domineering woman, and also displeased with Schlichtegroll's portrayal of her marriage. From sources such as these, one might conclude that the fantastic fiction of *Venus in Furs* was a barely embroidered history of the author's private life. In fact, it is important to keep in mind that the role of fantasy in both Sacher-Masoch's life and his literary work is so exceptionally pervasive that the distinction between fact and fiction is curiously problematic. Krafft-Ebing attempted to address the problem in a spirit of somewhat misplaced liberalism:

> As a man Sacher-Masoch can not lose anything in the estimation of his cultured fellow beings simply because he was afflicted with an anomaly of his sexual feelings. As an author he suffered severe injury so far as the influence and intrinsic merit of his work is concerned, for so long and whenever he eliminated his perversion from his literary efforts, he was a gifted writer, and as such would have achieved real greatness had he been actuated by normally sexual feelings.[17]

Krafft-Ebing evidently believed that the masochism of Sacher-Masoch severely vitiated his artistic work, despite being aware that the proposed elimination would have cost the author a part of his public. As Krafft-Ebing was the first to recognize, "Many perverts refer to this author as having given typical descriptions of their psychical conditions."[18] The professor of sexual pathology did not consider the possibility that what made a work like *Venus in Furs* a masterpiece might be precisely the author's working of his atypical romantic inclinations into a perversely persuasive, elegantly elaborate, psychically seductive literary fantasy.

Biographical research reveals that the relationship of Severin with Wanda was closely modeled on Sacher-Masoch's recently concluded connection with a young widow named Fanny von Pistor. He traveled with her to Italy, acting as her servant under the name of Gregor, in Polish livery, taking the third-class compartment in the train, while she, in first class, assumed the Slavic name of the "Princess Bogdanoff." In 1869 Sacher-Masoch signed a contract of slavery with Fanny von Pistor, with many of the same clauses that appeared the following year in the fictional contract, including the provision that the lady "promises to wear fur as often as practical and especially when being cruel." A photograph from that year shows her in furs, and him on his knees before her. Yet, if his life provided material for his novel, *Venus in Furs*, in turn, was reenacted in his life, and he went on to sign a contract of slavery with his own wife: "I commit myself on my word of honor to be the slave of Frau Wanda von Dunajew, in exact accordance with her demands, and to submit unresistingly to everything that she imposes on me."[19] The name "Wanda von Dunajew" was his own fictional invention, then adopted by his wife, and it was therefore difficult to determine whether his marriage entered into his fiction or his fiction became a part of his marriage.

Supposedly, the crushing conclusion of the novella, the brutal encounter with Wanda's Greek lover, had no basis in biographical experience. In fiction, this ultimate humiliation became the "cure" for Severin's masochism; in fact, Sacher-Masoch achieved no such cure, and spent the rest of his life in pursuit of both Venus and her male counterpart, the Apollonian Greek. Wanda, his wife, claimed to have only reluctantly acceded to her husband's exhortations to throw herself at other men. Just recovering from childbirth in Graz in 1875, she was distressed to find Sacher-Masoch in great excitement about a personal advertisement for romantic companionship placed by a gentleman in the Viennese press. "Wanda, we have found the Greek!" he cried, and when a photograph arrived showing "a handsome young man in Oriental costume," Sacher-Masoch was "electrified," and kept shouting, "The Greek! The Greek!" He could hardly wait for her to recover from her delivery so that she could go and seek out the stranger, and meanwhile commissioned for her a new cloak "not only trimmed but entirely lined with fur." Wanda complained that "it was extremely heavy—even when I was strong and in good health I could not stand to wear furs like this for long—they hurt my shoulders."[20] *Venus in Furs* leaves little room for doubt that the figure of the Greek reflected the homosexual aspect of Severin's fantasies:

> He *was* a handsome man, by God. No, more: he was a man such as I had never seen in the flesh. He stands in the Belvedere, hewn in marble, with the same slender and yet iron muscles, the same face, the same rippling curls. And what actually made him so peculiarly beautiful was that he wore no beard; and had his pelvis been less narrow, he might have been mistaken for a woman in male disguise . . . and that strange line around his mouth, the leonine lips that revealed a bit of the teeth and momentarily gave the face a touch of cruelty—
>
> Apollo flaying Marsyas. . . .
>
> Now I understood male Eros and admired Socrates for remaining virtuous with Alcibiades.[21]

The supposed cure which Severin undergoes at the hands of the Greek should perhaps be considered, in part, as Sacher-Masoch's reluctance to pursue further the homosexual implications of the encounter. In the author's life the pursuit of "the Greek" was always encountering obstacles, even in the case of an ardent male admirer who appeared under the name of "Anatole," and who may or may not have been mad King Ludwig of Bavaria. Just as

Sacher-Masoch felt compelled to deny any personal allegiance to Judaism, so also an unacknowledged sympathy with homosexuality marked another psychic site that he obviously found ambivalently compelling.

In *Venus in Furs* Sacher-Masoch artistically represents the frenzied romantic fantasies of Severin in relation to the classical deities of Venus and Apollo, each invoked in marble form as the Medici Venus and the Belvedere Apollo, each incarnated in the flesh in Wanda and the Greek. The statue of Venus, from her first sneezes, seems to rule with cruel purpose over the human emotional landscape, and Apollo turns out to be no less dangerous to his devotees. It would be possible to look for Sacher-Masoch's literary lineage in the classically inspired spirits of the eighteenth century, like Winckelmann, who sought the underlying principles of Greek sculpture in the "sublimely superhuman" form of the Apollo Belvedere, and Goethe, who, during his *Italian Journey*, contemplated the concept of beauty in the contours of the same statue.[22] More immediately, Sacher-Masoch followed the traces of nineteenth-century Romantic writers like Joseph von Eichendorff, whose story "The Marble Statue" brought Venus dangerously to life at the site of an ancient pagan temple, or Prosper Mérimée, whose "Venus of Ille" involved a statue menacing enough to commit murder when a man misvalued her divine elevation. Sacher-Masoch might also have thought of the thrall of Venus over Tannhäuser in Wagner's opera of the 1840s. There was even a curious convergence of interests with Nietzsche, whose *Birth of Tragedy* in 1872 articulated the conflict between Apollonian and Dionysian principles in ancient drama; interestingly, Wanda, as a votary of Venus, advocated pagan sensuality against the ascetic spirit of Christianity, offering an intimation of the themes that Nietzsche would later explore in the *Genealogy of Morals*. Indeed, Severin's identification of himself as a "suprasensualist" might be viewed in relation to the supermanly qualities that interested Nietzsche.

In 1967 the rock group the Velvet Underground reorchestrated the masochistic fantasies of Severin in the kinky rhythms of the song they called "Venus in Furs," featured on the famous Andy Warhol banana album. It was also in 1967 that the philosophical critic Gilles Deleuze, in an important essay on *Venus in Furs*, sought to delineate the radical differences in style and strategy between Sacher-Masoch and the Marquis de Sade, and argued against associating them within the same sado-masochistic complex. Deleuze emphasized the aestheticism of literary masochism, its attention to works of art and dependence upon the invocation of artistic tableaux. The novella not only focuses on statues, but also introduces paintings and even photographs to assist the staging of the masochistic fantasy. According to Deleuze, "Women become exciting when they are indistinguishable from cold statues in the moonlight or paintings in darkened rooms. *Venus* is set under the sign of Titian, with its mystical play of flesh, fur, and mirror, and the conjunction of cold, cruelty, and sentiment. The scenes in Masoch have of necessity a frozen quality, like statues or portraits; they are replicas of works of art."[23] The uncannily incantatory powers of these artifacts within the novella suggest that it may be interpreted as part of the genre that has been labeled the "fantastic" by the structuralist critic Tzvetan Todorov.[24] His concept of the fantastic stipulates interpretive suspense between supernatural explanation and illusionary imagination, as, for instance, when the reader remains uncertain about whether Sacher-Masoch's statues and paintings possess magical powers or whether they are imaginatively invested with such powers by the overwrought protagonists. The notion of the fantastic is particularly valuable for considering a work like *Venus in Furs*, which is so fundamentally concerned with the psychological play of fantasy. In this regard, one can also discern in Sacher-Masoch's work some of the same literary concerns that dominate the greatest novellas of the early twentieth century, such as Thomas Mann's *Death in Venice*, in which the hero is destroyed by dangerous romantic fantasies, framed in a struggle between Apollonian and Dionysian forces, or Arthur Schnitzler's *Traumnovelle*, in which dreams and fantasies seem to overwhelm the urban bourgeois reality of the susceptible protagonist.

"The most common and the most significant of all the perversions—the desire to inflict pain upon the sexual object, and its reverse—received from Krafft-Ebing the names of sadism and masochism," wrote Sigmund Freud in his pathbreaking *Three Essays on the Theory of Sexuality*, published in 1905.[25] Sacher-Masoch had died ten years before, in 1895, and Freud did not mention him at all, as if the concept of masochism had already completely displaced the literary oeuvre which inspired its formulation. Krafft-Ebing had made use of Sacher-Masoch's name in order to generalize about a set of case histories, treating the author's fiction in relation to those psychopathological cases. In fact, *Venus in Furs* gives some encouragement to such an approach, inasmuch as Sacher-Masoch sometimes presents Severin as a sort of case history.

> I was perched on a footstool at the feet of my Goddess, talking about my childhood.
> "And by then all these singular tendencies had already crystallized in you?" asked Wanda.
> "Yes indeed. I can't remember ever not having them. Even in my cradle, as my mother subsequently told me, I was *suprasensual*."[26]

Continuing to take an analytic interest in his case, Wanda asks, "How did you develop this passion for fur?" Severin answers, "I already showed it as a child." Furthermore, in the manner of the mock case history, *Venus in Furs* concludes with the patient proclaiming his cure. Indeed, Wanda, in a final letter to Severin, insists that she had always been thinking along therapeutic lines: "I hope that you were healed under my whip; the therapy was cruel but radical."[27] The cure is perhaps the least persuasive part of the fiction, as unconvincing as the Marquis de Sade's occasional claim that he was making a case for virtue by demonstrating the monstrosity of vice. Sacher-Masoch's literary fantasies were too evidently aimed at the artful gratification of himself, his hero, and perhaps his readers, for anyone to credit the conceit that Severin's case history was supposed to publicize a cure for sexual pathology.

The narrative critic Dorrit Cohn, considering Freud's case histories, has demonstrated his sensitivity to the distinction between fictional and historical writing in the representation of his patients' cases.[28] Freud further deferred to that distinction when he adopted Krafft-Ebing's abstract term for "masochism" without reference to Sacher-Masoch or his work. Rather, when Freud offered a literary instance of masochism in the *Three Essays,* he preferred to cite the most celebrated nonfictional case: "Ever since Jean-Jacques Rousseau's *Confessions,* it has been well known to all educationalists that the painful stimulation of the skin of the buttocks is one of the erotogenic roots of the passive instinct of cruelty (masochism)."[29] It was in the *Three Essays* that Freud, the greatest Habsburg theorist of sexuality, incorporated the concept of masochism into the broader intellectual framework of psychoanalysis. While Sacher-Masoch believed that his own tastes were widespread, and Krafft-Ebing confirmed that the various perversions were not uncommon, Freud went further: "In view of what was now seen to be the wide dissemination of tendencies to perversion we were driven to the conclusion that a disposition to perversions is an original and universal disposition of the human sexual instinct and that normal sexual behavior is developed out of it as a result of organic changes and psychical inhibitions occurring in the course of maturation." Freud found this universal perversity in "the multifariously perverse sexual disposition of childhood," which he also sometimes called "polymorphous perversity."[30] Psychoanalytic theory thus made masochism, along with sadism, a basic element of the human instinctual heritage.

In the case of the Wolf Man, who happened to be Russian, Freud explored the relation of masochism to sadism, castration anxiety, homosexuality, Christianity, and, of course, the Oedipal drama: "In his sadism he maintained his ancient identification with his father; but in his masochism he chose him as a sexual object." In "The Economic Problem of Masochism" Freud argued that although the "pleasure principle" could make masochism appear "incomprehensible," masochistic impulses were closely related to the death instinct. In "A Child Is Being Beaten" Freud remarked that "a sense of guilt is invariably the factor that transforms sadism into masochism," and also explored the ways in which beating fantasies appeared to be conditioned by the Oedipus complex in both men and women. For Freud, the woman whose sexual fantasies are about bondage and beating, however deviously they may be revised or projected, is always governed by "the original phantasy in the case of the girl, 'I am being beaten (i.e. I am loved) by my father.' "[31] Freud's conception of masochism thus inevitably reflected both the intellectual insights and the cultural biases of psychoanalysis as a whole. By interpreting perversion as part of the "universal disposition of the human sexual instinct," Freud made psychoanalytic sense of masochism, borrowing the term from Krafft-Ebing, while effacing the original significance of Sacher-Masoch.

In the end Severin, claiming to be cured of his masochism, declares that from now on he intends to wield the whip: "Imagine the effect, however, on our fine, high-strung, hysterical ladies . . ."[32] Thus Sacher-Masoch's final impulse was to set Severin loose, with a whip, among the high-strung bourgeoisie of Habsburg society, in the hysterical echelons of Freud's female patients, whether to stimulate their sense of sexual fantasy or shock them into complete collapse. Unmistakably, Sacher-Masoch regarded such a scenario in a comic spirit, and not with the requisite seriousness that Freud would bring to hysteria at the end of the century. It is Sacher-Masoch's sense of play, evident from the first moment Venus sneezes, that makes him seem most alien to the serious studies of psychology, sex, and perversion, whether of Krafft-Ebing or of Freud. Venus in Furs was supposed to be part of a much larger literary project that Sacher-Masoch portentously called The Testament of Cain, but Severin seems almost lighthearted in his pursuit of torment. Sacher-Masoch, who died in the same year that Freud published the Studies on Hysteria, invoked a Habsburg genius of an altogether different spirit when he proudly pointed out that he shared his birthday, January 27,

INTRODUCTION   xxvii

with Wolfgang Amadeus Mozart. Whatever the disparities of genius, one certainly feels that Sacher-Masoch in his fiction, like
Mozart in his music, was having fun. Severin is often attuned to
the comic aspects of his position, and even in the supremely
brutal climactic scene he declares, "The situation was dreadfully funny—I would have laughed myself if it hadn't been so
desperately dismal, so degrading for me." Sacher-Masoch took
perverse pleasure in purveying his romantic fantasies, however
humiliating, in *Venus in Furs*, and the author's pleasure still com-
municates itself to a polymorphously perverse public. "You've
aroused my most cherished fantasy," says Severin to Wanda, but,
a little later, she reformulates the issue, addressing him: "You've
corrupted my imagination, inflamed my blood. I'm starting to
enjoy all those things."[33] More than a century after the author's
death, and long after the dissolution of the Habsburg monarchy
which conditioned his literary life, Sacher-Masoch's masterpiece
Venus in Furs continues to corrupt the imagination by its irre-
sistibly seductive and artfully inflammatory sense of fantasy.

NOTES

1. Richard von Krafft-Ebing, *Psychopathia Sexualis*, trans. Franklin S.
   Klaf (New York: Arcade Publishing, 1998), pp. 87, 95–96, 109–10,
   123, 125–26.
2. *Venus in Furs*, p. 37.
3. Wanda von Sacher-Masoch, *The Confessions of Wanda von Sacher-
   Masoch*, trans. Marian Phillips, Caroline Hébert, and V. Vale (San
   Francisco: Re/Search Publications, 1990), pp. 11–12.
4. *Venus in Furs*, p. 82.
5. *Venus in Furs*, pp. 95–96.
6. *Venus in Furs*, p. 39.
7. Bernard Michel, *Sacher-Masoch* (Paris: Editions Robert Laffont,
   1989), p. 181.
8. Krafft-Ebing, p. 98.
9. Leopold von Sacher-Masoch, *A Light for Others and Other Jewish
   Tales from Galicia*, trans. Michael T. O'Pecko (Riverside, Calif.:
   Ariadne Press, 1994), p. 7.

10. Leopold von Sacher-Masoch, *Souvenirs: Autobiographische Prosa* (Munich: Belleville, 1985), pp. 16–17.

11. Sacher-Masoch, *Souvenirs*, pp. 23–24.

12. *Venus in Furs*, pp. 7, 12, 40–41.

13. *Venus in Furs*, pp. 3, 9.

14. Marquis de Custine, *Empire of the Czar: A Journey Through Eternal Russia* (New York: Anchor Books, 1990), p. 96.

15. Carl Felix von Schlichtegroll, *Sacher-Masoch und der Masochismus* (Dresden: Dohrn, 1901), p. 5; Michel, pp. 130–31.

16. *Venus in Furs*, pp. 50, 52, 73, 75.

17. Krafft-Ebing, p. 87.

18. Krafft-Ebing, p. 113.

19. Appendix, *Venus in Furs*, pp. 121, 122.

20. Wanda von Sacher-Masoch, p. 37.

21. *Venus in Furs*, pp. 96–97.

22. Alex Potts, *Flesh and the Ideal: Winckelmann and the Origins of Art History* (New Haven, Conn.: Yale University Press, 1994), p. 118.

23. Gilles Deleuze, "Coldness and Cruelty," in *Masochism* (New York: Zone Books, 1991), p. 69.

24. Tzvetan Todorov, *The Fantastic: A Structural Approach to a Literary Genre*, trans. Richard Howard (Ithaca, N.Y.: Cornell University Press, 1975), pp. 24–40.

25. Sigmund Freud, *Three Essays on the Theory of Sexuality*, in *The Standard Edition of the Complete Psychological Works of Sigmund Freud*, ed. James Strachey, vol. 7 (London: The Hogarth Press, 1953), p. 157.

26. *Venus in Furs*, p. 30.

27. *Venus in Furs*, pp. 35, 118.

28. Dorrit Cohn, "Freud's Case Histories and the Question of Fictionality," in *The Distinction of Fiction* (Baltimore: Johns Hopkins University Press, 1999), pp. 38–57.

29. Freud, *Three Essays*, p. 193.

30. Freud, *Three Essays*, pp. 231, 239.

31. Freud, *From the History of an Infantile Neurosis* (Wolf Man), in *The Standard Edition*, vol. 17, p. 63; "The Economic Problem of Masochism," in *The Standard Edition*, vol. 19, pp. 159, 164; " 'A Child Is Being Beaten': A Contribution to the Study of the Origin of Sexual Perversions," in *The Standard Edition*, vol. 17, pp. 189, 202.

32. *Venus in Furs*, p. 119.

33. *Venus in Furs*, pp. 114–115, 37, 38.

SUGGESTIONS FOR FURTHER READING

Unfortunately, very little of Sacher-Masoch's work is available in English translation. There is a good English edition of Sacher-Masoch's Jewish tales, called *A Light for Others and Other Jewish Tales from Galicia*, translated by Michael T. O'Pecko (Riverside, Calif.: Ariadne Press, 1994). There is also a peculiarly published English edition of Wanda's memoirs, *The Confessions of Wanda von Sacher-Masoch* (San Francisco: Re/Search Publications, 1990). The 12th edition of Krafft-Ebing's *Psychopathia Sexualis* is available in English (New York: Arcade Publishing, 1998), with a lengthy discussion of masochism (pp. 86–143). There is an English biography of Sacher-Masoch, called *The First Masochist*, by James Cleugh (London: Anthony Blond, 1967), but the more recent French biography, *Sacher-Masoch*, by Bernard Michel (Paris: Editions Robert Laffont, 1989) is much better. The German edition of Sacher-Masoch's autobiographical writings (which were originally published in French) is called *Souvenirs: Autobiographische Prosa* (Munich: Belleville, 1985). The essay by Gilles Deleuze on *Venus in Furs*, "Coldness and Cruelty," is a classic of criticism, published in *Masochism* (New York: Zone Books, 1991). There are also interesting scholarly essays by Gertrud Lenzer, "On Masochism: A Contribution to the History of a Phantasy and Its Theory" (*Signs*, Winter 1975, vol. 1, no. 2, pp. 277–324); and David Biale, "Masochism and Philosemitism: The Strange Case of Leopold von Sacher-Masoch" (*Journal of Contemporary History*, vol. 17, 1982, pp. 305–23). There are good brief treatments of Sacher-Masoch in Bram Dijkstra's *Idols of Perversity: Fantasies of Feminine Evil in Fin-de-Siècle Culture* (New York: Oxford University Press,

1986), in chap. 11; and in William Johnston, *The Austrian Mind: An Intellectual and Social History* (Berkeley: University of California Press, 1972), in chap. 15. For background on Eastern Europe there is Larry Wolff, *Inventing Eastern Europe: The Map of Civilization on the Mind of the Enlightenment* (Stanford, Calif.: Stanford University Press, 1994), chap. 2, "Possessing Eastern Europe: Sexuality, Slavery, and Corporal Punishment."

VENUS IN FURS

*God did punish him and deliver him
into a woman's hands.*

Judith 16:7

I had a charming guest.

Opposite me, by the massive Renaissance fireplace, sat Venus: not, mind you, some demimondaine who, like Mademoiselle Cleopatra, had taken the pseudonym of Venus in her war against the enemy sex. No: my visitor was the Goddess of Love—in the flesh.

She sat in an easy chair after fanning up a crackling fire, and the reflections of red flames licked her pale face with its white eyes and, from time to time, her feet when she tried to warm them.

Her head was wonderful despite the dead stone eyes, but that was all I saw of her. The sublime being had wrapped her marble body in a huge fur and, shivering, had curled up like a cat.

"I don't understand, dear Madam," I cried. "It's really not cold anymore; for the past two weeks we've had the most glorious spring weather. You're obviously high-strung."

"Thank you for your spring, but no thanks," she said in a deep stone voice and instantly sneezed two divine sneezes in quick succession. "I truly can't stand it and I'm beginning to grasp—"

"Grasp what, dear Madam?"

"I'm beginning to believe the unbelievable and comprehend the incomprehensible. I suddenly understand Germanic female virtue and German philosophy, and I'm no longer amazed that you northerners are unable to love—indeed, haven't got the foggiest notion of what love is."

"Permit me, Madam," I replied, flaring up. "I have truly given you no occasion."

3

"Well, you—" The divine being sneezed a third time and shrugged with inimitable grace. "That's why I've always been lenient with you and even visit you every so often although I promptly catch cold each time despite my many furs. Do you recall our first meeting?"

"How could I forget it?" I said. "You had rich, brown curls and brown eyes and red lips, but I immediately recognized you by the contours of your face and by that marble pallor—you always wore a violet velvet jacket lined with vair."

"Yes, you were quite enamored of that attire, and what a good pupil you were."

"You taught me what love is. Your cheerful divine service made me forget two thousand years."

"And how incomparably faithful I was to you!"

"Well, as for being faithful—"

"Ungrateful wretch!"

"I won't reproach you. You may be a godly woman, but you're a woman all the same, and when it comes to love you are as cruel as any woman."

"What you call 'cruel,'" the Goddess of Love vividly retorted, "is precisely the element of sensuality and cheerful love—which is a woman's nature. She must give herself to whatever or whomever she loves and must love anything that pleases her."

"Is there any greater cruelty for the lover than the beloved woman's infidelity?"

"Ah," she countered, "we are faithful as long as we love, but you men demand that women be faithful without love and give ourselves without joy. Who is the cruel one here? The woman or the man? On the whole, you northerners take love too earnestly, too seriously. You talk about duties, when all that should count is pleasure."

"Yes, Madam, but then we have very respectable and virtuous emotions and lasting relationships."

"And yet," Madam broke in, "that eternally restless, eternally unquenched desire for naked paganism, that love that is the supreme joy, that is divine serenity itself—those things are useless for you moderns, you children of reflection. That sort of love wreaks havoc on you. *As soon as you wish to be natural you become common.* To you Nature seems hostile, you have turned us laughing Greek deities into demons and me into a devil. All you can do is exorcise me and curse me or else sacrifice yourselves, slaughter yourselves in bacchanalian madness at my altar. And if any of you ever has the courage to kiss my red lips, he then goes on a pilgrimage to Rome, barefoot and in a penitent's shirt, and expects flowers to blossom from his withered staff,[1] while roses, violets, and myrtles sprout constantly under my feet—but their fragrance doesn't agree with you. So just stay in your northern fog and Christian incense. Let us pagans rest under the rubble, under the lava. Do not dig us up. Pompeii, our villas, our baths, our temples were not built for you people! You need no gods! We freeze in your world!" The beautiful marble lady coughed and drew the dark sable pelts more snugly around her shoulders.

"Thank you for the lesson in classical civilization," I replied. "But you cannot deny that in your serene and sunny world man and woman are natural-born enemies as much as in our foggy world. You cannot deny that love lasts for only a brief moment, uniting two beings as a single being that is capable of only one thought, one sensation, one will—only to drive these two persons even further apart. And then—you know this better than I—the person who doesn't know how to subjugate will all too quickly feel the other's foot on the nape of his neck—"

"And as a rule it is the man who feels the woman's foot," cried Madam Venus with exuberant scorn, "which you, in turn, know better than I."

"Of course, and that is precisely why I have no illusions."

"You mean you are now my slave without illusions, so that I can trample you ruthlessly!"

"Madam!"

"Don't you know me by now? Yes, I am *cruel*—since you take so much pleasure in that word—and am I not entitled to be cruel? Man desires, woman is desired. That is woman's entire but decisive advantage. Nature has put man at woman's mercy through his passion, and woman is misguided if she fails to make him her subject, her slave, no, her toy and ultimately fails to laugh and betray him."

"Your principles, dear Madam—" I indignantly broke in.

"—Are based on thousands of years of experience," she sarcastically retorted, her white fingers playing in the dark fur. "The more devoted the woman is, the more quickly the man sobers up and becomes domineering. But the crueler and more faithless she is, the more she mistreats him, indeed the more wantonly she plays with him, the less pity she shows him, the more she arouses the man's lascivious yearning to be loved and worshiped by the woman. It's always been like that in all times, from Helen and Delilah to Catherine the Great and Lola Montez."

"I cannot deny," I said, "that nothing excites a man more than the sight of a beautiful, voluptuous, and cruel female despot who capriciously changes her favorites, reckless and rollicking—"

"And wears a fur to boot!" cried the Goddess.

"What do you mean?"

"I'm familiar with your predilection."

"But you know," I broke in, "you've grown very coquettish since last we met."

"How so, if I may ask?"

"In that nothing brings out your white body more splendidly that those dark furs, and you—"

The Goddess laughed.

"You're dreaming," she exclaimed, "wake up!" And her marble hand grabbed my arm. "Wake up!" her voice rang firmly.

I laboriously opened my eyes.

I saw the hand that was shaking me, but this hand was suddenly as brown as bronze, and the voice was the heavy whiskey voice of my Cossack, who was standing before me at his full height of almost six feet.

"C'mon, get up," the valiant man went on, "it's a cryin' shame."

"And why a shame?"

"A shame to fall asleep fully dressed, and while readin' a book at that!" He snuffed the guttered candles and picked up the volume that had slipped from my hand. "A book by—" He opened it: "By Hegel.[2] C'mon! It's high time we drove over to Herr Severin—he's expectin' us for tea."

"A strange dream," said Severin when I was done. He propped his arms on his knees, his face on his finely and delicately veined hands, and was lost in thought.

I knew that he would sit motionless for a long time, scarcely breathing, and such was the case. But for me there was nothing peculiar about his behavior: having been close friends with him for almost three years now, I was accustomed to all his eccentricities. And eccentric he *was*—there is no denying it—though he was far from being the dangerous fool that he was regarded as not just by his neighbors but throughout the district of Kolomea. I found his personality not only interesting but (and that was why many people also considered me a bit crazy) extremely likable.

For a Galician[3] nobleman and landowner and for a man of his age (he was barely over thirty), he displayed a conspicuous sobriety, a certain earnestness, even pedantry. He lived according to a minutely implemented, half-philosophical, half-practical system, virtually by the clock, and not only that, but also by the thermometer, barometer, aerometer, hydrometer, by Hippocrates, Hufeland, Plato, Kant, Knigge, and Lord Chesterfield. Yet at times he suffered vehement fits of passion and acted as if he were about to smash his head through the wall. At such moments everyone preferred to keep out of his way.

As if making up for his silence, the flames in the fireplace sang, the big and venerable samovar sang, and the grandfather chair sang as I rocked to and fro, smoking my cigar; and the cricket in the old wall sang too, and my eyes swept over the outlandish implements, the animal skeletons, the stuffed birds, the globes, the plaster casts that had accumulated in Severin's room. My eyes then happened to linger on a painting that I had seen often enough; yet today, in the red glow of the fire, it had an indescribable impact on me.

It was a large oil painting in the intense colors and robust manner of the Belgian school; its subject was odd enough. A beautiful woman, with a sunny smile on her fine face, with rich, classically knotted hair covered with white powder like a soft frost: naked in a dark fur, she reclined on a sofa, leaning on her left arm, her right hand playing with a whip, her bare foot casually propped on the man, who lay before her like a slave, like a dog. And this man, who revealed salient but well-shaped features infused with brooding melancholy and devoted passion, this man, who peered up at her with the burning, enraptured eyes of a martyr, this man, who served as a footstool for her feet—this man was Severin, but beardless and apparently ten years younger.

"*Venus in Furs!*" I cried, pointing to the picture. "That was how I saw her in my dreams."

"So did I," said Severin, "except that I dreamed my dream with open eyes."

"How?"

"Oh! It's a foolish story."

"The painting obviously inspired my dream," I went on. "Do please tell me, however, in what way it played a role in your life and, as I can imagine, perhaps a very crucial role. I look forward to the details."

"Just view its counterpart," my bizarre friend retorted without heeding my words.

The counterpart was an excellent copy of Titian's renowned *Venus with Mirror* in the Dresden Gallery.

"Well, what are you driving at?"

Severin stood up and pointed at the fur in which Titian had ensconced his Goddess of Love.

"This too is *Venus in Furs*," he said with a fine smile. "I don't think the old Venetian had any ulterior motive. He simply did a portrait of some aristocratic Messalina and was courteous enough to let Cupid hold the mirror in which she examines her majestic charms with cold satisfaction—though his task seems more like a chore to him. This is a work of painted flattery. Later on, some 'connoisseur' of the rococo dubbed the lady Venus, and the female despot's fur, in which Titian's beautiful model is wrapped probably more out of fear of sniffles than out of chastity, has become a symbol of the tyranny and cruelty intrinsic to a woman and her beauty.

"But enough. The painting, as it now looks, seems like the most piquant satire on our love. Venus, who, in the abstract north, in the icy Christian world, has to slip into a large, heavy fur to avoid catching cold."

Severin laughed and lit another cigarette.

Just then the door opened and a pretty, buxom blonde with smart, friendly eyes and in a black silk robe entered, bringing us cold meat and eggs for our tea. Severin took one of the eggs and broke it open with a knife. "Haven't I told you I want them soft-boiled?" he cried with a vehemence that made the young woman tremble.

"But dear Sevtshu—" she said anxiously.

"Don't call me Sevtshu!" he yelled. "You must obey, obey, do you understand," and he yanked down the knout that was hanging on a nail next to his weapons.

The pretty woman fearfully bolted from the room like a doe.

"Just you wait, I'll get you yet!" he hollered after her.

"But Severin," I said, putting my hand on his arm, "how can you treat that pretty young thing like this?"

"Now just look at her," he replied, winking humorously. "If I had flattered her, she would have thrown a noose around my neck. But this way, because I rear her with the knout, she adores me."

"Oh, come on!"

"You come on! That's how you have to train women."

"Live like a pasha in your harem for all I care, but don't feed me any theories—"

"Why not?" he cried briskly. "Nowhere is Goethe's dictum, 'You must be hammer or anvil,' more relevant than in the relationship between man and woman. And Madam Venus even admitted that to you in your dream. Woman's power lies in Man's passion, and she knows how to make use of it if man isn't careful. His only choice is to be woman's tyrant or slave. The instant he gives in, he already has his head in a yoke and he will feel the whip."

"Strange maxims!"

"No maxims, just experience," he retorted with a nod. "*I was seriously whipped*, I'm cured. Would you like to read about it?"

He rose and, going to a massive desk, produced a small manuscript, which he placed before me on the table.

"You've asked about that painting. I've owed you an explanation for a long time. Here—read!"

Severin sat down by the fireplace with his back toward me and seemed to be dreaming with open eyes. The room was silent again, and again the flames in the fireplace sang, as did the samovar, and the cricket in the old wall, and I opened the manuscript and read:

"*Confessions of a Suprasensual Man.*" The epigraph in the margin was a variation of Mephistopheles' well-known verses from *Faust*:

> You suprasensual sensual suitor,
> A woman leads you by the nose!

I turned over the title page and read: "The following text is compiled from my journal of that period since the past can never be depicted without bias; in this way, everything has its fresh colors, the colors of the present."

Gogol, the Russian Molière says—indeed where? Well, somewhere—that the true comic muse is the one with tears running down under her laughing mask.

A wonderful statement!

So I feel rather odd while writing this. The air seems filled with an arousing scent of flowers, numbing my mind and making my head ache. The smoke in the fireplace curls and masses into figures: small, gray-bearded goblins, who point mockingly at me, while chubby-cheeked cupids ride on the arms of my chair and on my lap. And I can't help smiling, indeed laughing raucously as I record my adventures; and yet I am writing not with mundane ink but with the red blood that drips from my heart; for all its long-healed wounds have reopened, and my heart stings and suffers, and now and then a tear falls on the paper.

The days were crawling by lethargically in the small Carpathian resort. One saw nobody and was seen by nobody. It was boring enough to pen an idyll. I had sufficient leisure to come up with a whole gallery of paintings, to furnish a theater with an entire season of new plays, to supply a dozen virtuosi with concertos, trios, and duets. But—what am I saying?—ultimately I did nothing much more than stretch the canvas, straighten out the pages, line the music sheets, for I was—Ah! No false modesty, my friend Severin. Lie to others; but you no longer quite manage to lie to yourself. Well, I was nothing more than a dilettante: a dilettante in painting, in poetry, in music, and in a few more of the so-called unprofitable arts, which nowadays, however, assure their masters the income of a cabinet minister, nay, a minor potentate. And above all, I was a dilettante in life.

Until then, I had lived as I had painted and versified—that is, I never got far beyond priming a canvas, beyond penning an outline, a first act, a first stanza. There are simply people who start all sorts of things and yet never finish any of them. And that was the kind of person I was.

But what am I nattering for?!

Let me get to the point:

I lay in my window and found the nest I was despairing in so infinitely poetic: how lovely the view of the blue wall of lofty mountains enveloped in the golden haze of the sun and crisscrossed by torrents winding like silver ribbons. And how clear and blue the sky, into which the snowy peaks towered; and how green and fresh the wooded slopes, the meadows, where tiny herds were grazing, down to the yellow of the billows of grain where the harvesters stood and bent and rose again.

The house I was staying in was located in a kind of park or forest or wilderness—whatever one wishes to call it—and was very isolated.

No one lived here except for myself, a widow from Lwów, and the proprietress Madam Tartakowska, a little old lady who kept growing older and littler by the day, plus an old dog with one lame foot, and a young cat that always played with a ball of yarn—and the yarn belonged, I assumed, to the beautiful widow.

She was, I heard, truly beautiful, the widow, and still very young, at most twenty-four, and very rich. She lived one flight up while I lived on the ground floor. She always kept her green blinds drawn and had a balcony completely overgrown with green vines. I, however, had my dear, cozy, honeysuckle gazebo, where I read and wrote and painted and sang like a bird in the branches. I could look up at the balcony. Sometimes I really did look up, and then from time to time a white gown up there shimmered through the dense, green net.

Actually I had very little interest in the beautiful woman up there, since I was in love with another—indeed, very unhappily in love, far more unhappily than Sir Toggenburg or the chevalier in *Manon Lescaut*,[4] for my beloved was made of stone.

In the garden, in the small wilderness, there was a charming little meadow, where a couple of tame deer grazed peacefully. And in that meadow there was a stone statue of Venus. The original, I believe, is in Florence. This Venus was the most beautiful woman I had ever seen.

Now that didn't mean very much, of course, for I had seen few beautiful women, indeed few women at all, and in regard to love I was a mere dilettante who never got beyond the priming, beyond the first act.

But why speak in superlatives—as if something that is beautiful could be surpassed?

Enough: this Venus was beautiful, and I loved her as passionately, as morbidly and profoundly, as insanely as a man can love only a woman who responds to his love with an eternally consistent, eternally calm stone smile. Yes, I literally worshiped her.

Often, when the sun brooded in the woods, I would lie reading under the leafy canopy of a young beech; often I visited my
cold, cruel beloved at night too, kneeling before her, pressing my
face into the cold stones under her feet, and praying to her.

There is no describing the way the moon, now waxing, rose
and floated through the trees and dipped the meadow in a silvery
glow, and the Goddess then stood as if transfigured and seemed
to bathe in the soft moonlight.

Once, while returning from my worship, I was walking along
a garden path leading to the house when I abruptly saw—sepa-
rated from me only by the green gallery of trees—a female figure, white as stone, shining in the moonlight. I felt as if the
beautiful marble woman had taken pity on me and had come
alive and followed me. But then I was seized with a nameless
fear, my heart was ready to burst, and instead of—

Well, I was a dilettante after all. I bogged down as usual in the
second verse. No! Quite the contrary! I didn't bog down. I ran
as fast as I could run.

What luck! A Jew who dealt in photographs somehow con-
trived to get me the portrait of my beloved: this small work on
paper was a reproduction of Titian's *Venus with Mirror*. What a
woman! I wanted to write a poem. No! I took the picture and
wrote on it: *Venus in Furs*.

You freeze while arousing flames. Just wrap yourself in your
despotic fur; whom does it suit if not you, cruel Goddess of
Beauty and Love?!

And after a while I added a few Goethe verses, which I had recently found in his paralipomena to *Faust*:

To Cupid

> *His arrows, they are only claws,*
> *His wings a pair of lies,*
> *His horns are hidden by the wreath,*
> *He is, we must surmise,*
> *Like all the Gods of ancient Greece,*
> *A devil in disguise.*

Then I placed the picture before me on the table, leaning it against a book and viewing it.

I was both delighted and horrified by the hardness, the severity of the marble countenance, by the icy coquetry with which the splendid woman drapes her charms in the dark sable furs.

I picked up the quill again. Here is what I wrote:

"To love, to be loved—what happiness! And yet how the brightness fades against the tortured bliss of worshiping a woman who turns us into a plaything, the bliss of being the slave of a beautiful female tyrant who ruthlessly tramples us underfoot. Even Samson, the hero, the giant gave himself over once again to Delilah, who had already betrayed him, and she betrayed him once again, and the Philistines bound him up before her and put out his eyes, which, drunk with rage and love, rested on the beautiful traitress until the very last moment."

I had breakfast in my honeysuckle gazebo and read the Book of Judith and envied the grim hero Holofernes for the queenly woman who chopped his head off and for the gory beauty of his death.

"God did punish him and deliver him into a woman's hands."

That verse struck me.

How ungallant these Jews are, I thought. And their God—He could pick more decent expressions when speaking about the fair sex.

"*God did punish him and deliver him into a woman's hands*," I repeated to myself. Well, what could I possibly do to make Him punish me?

For God's sake! Here was our landlady. She had again grown a bit smaller overnight. And up there, among the green vines and festoons, again the white gown. Was it Venus or the widow?

This time it was the widow, for Madame Tartakowska curtsied and, on the widow's behalf, asked to borrow something to read. I hurried into my room and pulled a few volumes together.

I recalled—too late—that my picture of Venus was in one of those volumes. Now the white woman up there had it along with my effusions.

What would she say about them?
I heard her laugh.
Was she laughing at me?

Full moon! There it was, peeping over the tops of the lower firs
that edged the park, and a silvery haze filled the terrace, the
clumps of trees, the entire landscape as far as the eye could see,
and the haze blurred softly into the distance like quivering wa-
ters.

I couldn't resist. Something was calling me, urging me so
strangely. I got dressed again and stepped into the garden.

I was drawn to the meadow, to her, my Goddess, my beloved.

The night was cool. I shivered. The air was heavy with the
smells of flowers and woods. It was intoxicating.

What a celebration! What music all around. A nightingale
sobbed. The stars glittered very faintly in the pale blue shimmer.
The meadow shone smooth as a mirror, as the ice covering a
pond.

Sublime and radiant was the statue of Venus.

Yet—what was that?

A huge, dark fur streamed from the marble shoulders of the
Goddess down to the soles of her feet—I stood rigid, gaping at
her, and again I was seized by that indescribable anxiety and I
fled.

I quickened my steps. Then I saw that I had missed my path,
and just as I was about to turn sideways into one of the green
trails, there, in front of me, on a stone bench, sat Venus, the
beautiful stone woman—no, the real Goddess of Love, with
warm blood and a throbbing pulse. Yes, she had come alive for
me, like that statue that had started breathing for her creator.[5]
True, the miracle was only half realized as yet: Her white hair
still glowed like stone and her white gown shimmered like
moonlight (or was it satin?) and the dark fur streamed from her
shoulders. But her lips were red by now and her cheeks were
taking on color, while her eyes shot two diabolical green shafts
into me—and then she laughed.

Her laugh was so bizarre, so—oh, it was indescribable, it took my breath away! I kept fleeing and had to stop every few yards and catch my breath, and that mocking laughter pursued me along the gloomy bower paths, across the bright lawns, into the thicket pierced only by a few moonbeams. I couldn't find my way, I wandered about, cold drops pearling on my forehead.

At last I halted and recited a brief monologue.

It went—well, one is always either very charming or very gross to oneself.

I said to myself: "Ass!"

That word had a powerful effect, like a magic formula releasing me and restoring my senses.

I was instantly calm.

Ecstatic, I repeated: "Ass!"

I now saw everything clear and sharp again: there was the fountain, there the path lined with boxwoods, there the house, toward which I slowly trudged.

Suddenly, once again, behind the silver embroidery of the green, moonlit wall: the white figure, the beautiful stone woman whom I worshiped, whom I feared, whom I was fleeing.

A few short leaps and I was in the house, catching my breath and pondering.

Just what was I really now: a small dilettante or a big fool?

A sultry morning: the air was dead, very spicy, agitating. I was sitting again in my honeysuckle gazebo and reading the *Odyssey,* the part about the attractive sorceress who turned her worshipers into beasts.[6] A delicious picture of ancient love.

The grass and the trees were rustling softly, and the leaves of my book were rustling, and the terrace was rustling too.

A woman's gown—

Here she was—Venus. But without furs. No, this time it was the widow, and yet—Venus. Oh! What a woman!

How she stood there in her white, airy morning robe, staring at me, and how poetic and graceful her fine shape! She wasn't tall, nor was she petite, and her face was more attractive, more *piquant* (in the sense of the days of the French marquises:

"naughty, racy") rather than strictly beautiful; and yet, how enchanting, what softness, what gracious mischief played about those full and not too small lips. Her skin was so infinitely delicate that the blue veins shimmered through everywhere, even through the muslin covering her arms and her bosom. How luxuriantly her red hair curled—yes, it was red, not blond or golden; and how demonically and yet charmingly it played around the back of her neck. And now her eyes struck me like bolts of green lightning. Yes, they were green, those eyes, with their indescribable gentle power; green, but green like precious stones, like deep, unfathomable mountain lakes.

She noticed my confusion, which even caused me to misbehave, for I remained seated and kept my cap on my head.

She smiled roguishly.

I finally stood up and greeted her. She came nearer and burst into a loud, almost childlike laughter. I stuttered as only a small dilettante or a big ass can stutter in such moments.

That was how we met.

The Goddess asked me for my name and told me hers: she was Wanda von Dunajew.

And she was really my Venus.

"But Madam, how did you ever hit on that?"

"Through the small picture that was inserted in one of your books—"

"I'd forgotten all about it."

"The strange remarks on the back—"

"Why strange?"

She looked at me. "I've always wanted to meet a real dreamer—for variety's sake. Well, all things considered, you strike me as one of the wildest."

"Dear Madam . . . in fact—" Again that obnoxious, asinine stuttering, plus my blushing, which may be appropriate in a boy of sixteen, but for me, who was almost ten years older. . . .

"You were afraid of me last night."

"Actually . . . however—but won't you have a seat?"

She sat down and relished my fear—for I dreaded her even

more now, in broad daylight—a charming scorn twitched around her upper lip.

"You view love and especially women," she began, "as something hostile, something against which you defend yourself, although in vain, something whose power over you, however, you feel as a sweet torment, a prickling cruelty: this is truly a modern attitude."

"You do not share it."

"I do not share it." She spoke quickly and decisively, shaking her head so vigorously that her curls flew up like red flames.

"I regard the cheerful sensuality of the Hellenes—a joy without pain—as an ideal that I strive for in my own life. For I don't believe in the love that is preached by Christianity, by the moderns, by the knights of the spirit. Yes, just take a look at me: I'm far worse than a heretic, I'm a pagan!

" 'You think the Goddess of Love really gave it much thought
"When Anchises pleased her in the Idaean Grove?'

"Those verses from Goethe's *Roman Elegies* have always delighted me.

"In Nature there is only the love of the Heroic Age, 'when gods and goddesses loved.' In those days

" 'Desire followed the glance, pleasure followed desire.'

"Everything else is bogus, affected, dishonest. Christianity (whose gruesome emblem, the cross, I find horrifying) introduced something alien, inimical into Nature and her innocent drives.

"The struggle of the mind with the sensory world is the Gospel of the moderns. I want no part of it."

"Yes, your place would be on Mount Olympus, Madam," I replied. "But we moderns simply can't endure classical cheerfulness, least of all in love. We are shocked by the very thought of sharing a woman—even an Aspasia[7]—with others; we are as jealous as our God. Thus, the name of the beautiful Phryne has become a term of abuse among us.

"We would rather have a pale, sorry Holbein Virgin who belongs entirely to us than a classical Venus, no matter how divinely beautiful, if she loves Anchises today, Paris tomorrow, and Adonis the day after. And when Nature does triumph in us, when we abandon ourselves in burning passion to such a woman, her cheerful joie de vivre strikes us as demonic, as cruel, and we see our bliss as a sin that we must atone for."

"So you too are a fan of the modern woman, that poor, hysterical little female, who, in somnambular pursuit of her dream, her masculine ideal, fails to appreciate the best man and who, amid tearful fits, neglects her Christian duties every day, cheating and being cheated on, constantly seeking and choosing and rejecting, never happy, never making anyone else happy, and cursing fate instead of calmly admitting: 'I want to love and live as Helen and Aspasia lived.' Nature knows of no permanence in the male-female relationship."

"Dear Madam—"

"Let me finish. It is merely the egoism of the man, who wants to bury a woman like a treasure. All attempts at using vows, contracts, and holy ceremonies have failed to bring permanence into the most changeable aspect of changeable human existence, namely love. Can you deny that our Christian world is rotting?"

"But—"

"But you mean to say that the individual who rebels against the institutions of society is ostracized, stigmatized, stoned. Fine. I dare to try. My principles are quite pagan, I want to make the most of my existence. I can do without your hypocritical respect, I prefer happiness. The inventors of Christian marriage were correct in simultaneously inventing immortality. But I do not plan to live forever, and if everything for me as Wanda von Dunajew is finished here with my last breath, what do I care whether my pure spirit sings in the angelic choirs or my dust billows into new shapes? Once I no longer exist as I am, out of what consideration should I then forgo anything? Should I belong to a man I don't love simply because I used to love him? No, I forgo nothing, I love any man who appeals to me and I make any man who loves me happy. Is that ugly? No, it is at least far more beautiful than my cruelly delighting in the tortures incited by my charms and my virtuously turning my back on the poor man who pines away for me. I am young, rich, and beautiful, and just as I am, I live cheerfully for pleasure and enjoyment."

While she spoke, with her eyes sparkling roguishly, I took hold of her hands without quite knowing what to do with them; but now, being the genuine dilettante that I was, I hastily let go.

"Your frankness," I said, "enthralls me, and not that alone—"

Again that wretched dilettantism, choking me, leaving me tongue-tied.

"What were you going to say?"

"I was going to say that—yes, I would want . . . Forgive me, dear Madam—I interrupted you."

"How so?"

A long pause. She was surely reciting a long monologue, which, translated into my language, could be summed up in a single word: "Ass."

"If you will permit me, dear Madam," I finally began. "How did you develop these—these notions?"

"Very simple. My father was a rationalist. Starting in the cradle, I was surrounded by plaster casts of ancient statues. At ten, I read *Gil Blas*, at twelve *La Pucelle*. Just as other children were friends with Tom Thumb, Bluebeard, and Cinderella, I counted Venus and Apollo, Heracles and Laocoön as my friends. My husband had a cheerful, sunny disposition; not even the incurable ailment that overcame him shortly after our wedding could ever darken his brow for long. The very night before his death he took me into his bed, and during the many months he sat dying in his wheelchair, he would often joke with me: 'Well, do you already have an admirer?' I turned crimson. 'Don't cheat on me,' he once added. 'I would find that ugly. Just get yourself a handsome man or rather several. You're a good wife, but you're still half a child, you need toys.'

"I probably don't have to tell you that I had no admirer during his lifetime. Enough though. He groomed me to become what I am: a Greek."

"A Goddess," I broke in.

She smiled. "Which Goddess?"

"Venus."

She wagged her finger at me and knitted her brows. "Ultimately a *Venus in Furs*. Just wait—I have a big, big fur which can cover you totally. I want to catch you in it as if it were a net."

"Do you actually believe," I said quickly, for I had had a thought that, ordinary and fatuous as it was, I considered a very good thought. "Do you believe that your ideas can be acted upon in our time, that Venus in her unclad beauty and serenity can stroll impunitively among railroads and telegraphs?"

"*Unclad* certainly not, but in furs," she cried, laughing. "Would you like to see mine?"

"And then—"

"What do you mean: 'then'?"

"Free, lovely, cheerful, and happy people as the Greeks were can exist only if they have *slaves*, who perform the prosaic business of everyday life for them and, above all, labor for them."

"Of course," she replied mischievously. "An Olympian Goddess like me requires a whole army of slaves. So be wary of me."

"Why?"

I myself was startled by the boldness with which I had blurted out that "why." She, however, was anything but startled. Her lips curled up slightly, exposing her small white teeth, and she then spoke casually as if about something hardly worth the mention. "Do you want to be my slave?"

"In love there is no equality," I replied, earnest and solemn. "If I must choose between domination and submission, it seems to me that it would be far more appealing to be the slave of a beautiful woman. But where can I find a woman who, instead of trying to gain control by means of petty cantankerousness, knows how to rule with calm and self-assurance, even severity?"

"Well, ultimately that wouldn't be so difficult."

"You believe—"

"I—for instance!" She laughed, leaning way back. "I have a talent for despotism—I also own the necessary furs. But last night you were seriously frightened of me!"

"Seriously."

"And now?"

"Now—I'm more frightened of you than ever!"

We were together every day, I and—Venus; together a good deal of the time. We took breakfast in my honeysuckle gazebo and tea in her small salon, and I had a chance to display all my minor, very minor talents. Why had I schooled myself in all sciences, tried my hand at all arts if I was unable to serve a petite and pretty woman? . . .

However, this woman was anything but petite and she impressed me quite enormously. One day I drew her portrait, and while drawing I now so clearly sensed how little our modern attire suited her cameo head. She had little of Rome but much of Greece in her features.

I wanted to paint her now as Psyche, now as Astarte,[8] depending on whether her eyes had that enthusiastic and spiritual look or that half-languishing and half-singeing, that weary and voluptuous look. But she wished only a portrait.

Well, I would give her a fur.

Ah! How could I possibly have any doubts as to who merited a princely fur if not she?

When we were together one evening, I read Goethe's *Roman Elegies* to her. Then I put the book down and improvised a few things. She appeared satisfied, indeed she hung on my every word, and her bosom trembled.

Or was I mistaken?

The rain throbbed mournfully against the panes, the fire in the hearth crackled with a wintry snugness, I felt so much at home with her. For an instant I had lost all respect for the beautiful woman and I kissed her hand, and she put up with it.

Then I sat at her feet and read her a little poem that I had penned for her.

Venus in Furs

Gracious, devilish, mythical lady.
Put your foot upon your slave,
Stretching out your marble body
Under myrtles and agaves.

Yes—and now more! This time I had really gotten beyond the
first stanza; but that evening she ordered me to give her the manuscript. I had no copy, and today, when I am writing on the basis
of my journal, I can remember only that first stanza.

It was a curious sensation that I was experiencing. I did not believe that I was in love with Wanda—at least, I had felt nothing
of that flash of lightning, that kindling of passion at our first
meeting. But I did sense that her extraordinary, truly divine
beauty was gradually laying magical snares around me. Nor was
I developing an emotional attachment to her; it was a physical
submission—slow but all the more thorough.
   My suffering increased every day, and she—she merely
smiled.

Today, for no apparent reason, she suddenly said, "You interest
me. Most men are so ordinary, with no élan, no poetry, but you
have a certain depth and enthusiasm, above all an earnestness
that pleases me. I could grow fond of you."

After a brief but intense storm, we walked over to the meadow
and the Venus statue. The soil was steaming all around, mists rising into the sky like fumes from a sacrifice, a shredded rainbow
floating in the air, trees still dripping, but sparrows and finches
were already flitting from branch to branch, twittering pertly as
if supremely delighted about something, and everything was imbued with a fresh scent. We couldn't walk across the meadow, for
it was still soaked, glowing in the sun like a small pond, with the
Goddess of Love rising from its rippling surface. Around her

head a swarm of gnats was dancing, radiant in the sun and hovering over her like an aureole.

Wanda enjoyed the charming scene, and since there were still puddles on the benches along the path, she leaned on my arm in order to rest a bit. She was suffused with a sweet fatigue, her eyes half-shut, her breath grazing my cheek.

I took hold of her hand and—I truly don't know how I managed—I asked her:

"Could you love me, Madam?"

"Why not?" she replied, and her calm, sunny gaze alighted on me, but not for long.

A moment later, I knelt before her, pressing my flaming face into the airy muslin of her robe.

"Why, Severin!" she cried. "This is indecent!"

But I seized her small foot and pressed my lips upon it.

"You're getting more and more indecent!" she cried, freeing herself and striding quickly toward the house while her darling slipper remained in my hand.

Was that an omen?

The whole next day, I did not dare approach her. Toward evening, when I was sitting in my gazebo, her piquant little head with its red hair suddenly emerged through the green garlands of her balcony. "Why don't you come up?" she impatiently called down to me.

I scurried up the stairs, but once there I again lost heart and I tapped very softly. Instead of saying "Come in," she opened the door and stood on the threshold.

"Where is my slipper?"

"It is—I have—I want—" I stuttered.

"Get it, and then we'll have tea and we'll chat."

When I returned, she was busy with the samovar. I solemnly placed the slipper on the table and stood in the corner like a child awaiting its punishment.

I noticed that her forehead was slightly contracted, and there was something rigorous, domineering about her mouth—something that fascinated me.

All at once she burst out laughing.

"So—you're really in love—with me?"

"Yes, and I'm suffering more than you think."

"You're suffering?" She laughed again.

I was indignant, embarrassed, destroyed, but it was all quite useless.

"Why?" she went on. "I'm fond of you, very fond of you." She gave me her hand and beamed at me in an exceedingly friendly way.

"And you want to be my wife?"

Wanda gave me a look—yes, what kind of look? A look, I believe, mainly of astonishment and with a trace of scorn.

"Where did you suddenly muster all this courage?" she said.

"Courage?"

"Yes, particularly the courage to take a wife, and especially me?" She raised the slipper aloft. "Have you made friends with it so quickly?" she said, alluding to our German expression for a henpecked husband: "*Pantoffelheld*," "slipper hero."

"But joking aside: Do you really want to marry me?"

"Yes."

"Well, Severin, this is serious business. I believe that you love me, and I love you too, and, even more important, we interest one another. There is no danger of our getting bored all that soon. But you know I'm a frivolous woman, and that is precisely why I take marriage very seriously; and if I assume obligations, I want to be able to abide by them. But I'm afraid—no—you're sure to be hurt."

"I beg you, be honest with me," I countered.

"Well, to be honest: I don't believe I can love a man longer than . . ." She tilted her little head gracefully to one side and pondered.

"One year," I said.

"You must be joking! A month perhaps."

"With me, too?"

"Well, with you—two perhaps."

"Two months!" I screamed.

"Two months—that's a very long time."

"Madam, that's more than in Antiquity."

"You see? You can't stand the truth."

Wanda walked through the room, then leaned against the fireplace and gazed at me, her arm resting on the mantelpiece.

"What am I going to do with you?"

"Whatever you like," I answered, resigned, "whatever gives you pleasure."

"How inconsistent!" she cried. "First you want me as your wife and now you give yourself to me as a toy."

"Wanda—I love you."

"Then we're back where we started. You love me and want me as your wife. But I don't care to remarry, because I doubt that my and your feelings will be permanent."

"What if I want to take the chance?" I rejoined.

"Then it all depends on whether I want to take the chance with you," she murmured. "I can well imagine belonging to one man for life, but it would have to be a total man, a man who commands my respect, who subjugates me with the power of who and what he is—do you understand? And every man—I know this—turns weak, pliant, ridiculous as soon as he's in love. He puts himself in the woman's hands, kneels before her—whereas I can love only the man before whom *I* would kneel. But I've grown so fond of you that I want to try it with you."

I plunged to her feet.

"My goodness! You're already kneeling," she taunted me. "That's a good start." And when I stood up again, she continued: "I'll give you a year to win me over, to convince me that we are suited to each other, that we can live together. If you succeed, I'll be your wife, Severin—a wife who will perform her duties rigorously and conscientiously. During this year we will live as if in a marriage—"

The blood rushed to my head.

Her eyes likewise suddenly blazed up. "We will live together," she went on, "share all our habits, in order to see whether we can find ourselves in one another. *I grant you all the rights of a husband, an admirer, a friend!* Are you satisfied with that?

"I have to be, I guess."

"You don't have to be."

"Then I want to—"

"Excellent. That's the way a man speaks. Here is my hand."

For ten days I was never away from her for even an hour, except at night. I could constantly look into her eyes, hold her hands, listen to her speak, accompany her everywhere. My love was like a profound, a bottomless abyss, into which I kept sinking deeper and deeper, from which nothing could save me.

We spent an afternoon on the meadow, at the feet of the Venus statue. I was picking flowers and tossing them into Wanda's lap, and she was binding them into wreaths for adorning our Goddess.

Suddenly Wanda gave me such a peculiar, bewildering look that my passion blazed over my head like flames. Losing control of myself, I threw my arms around her and clung to her lips and she—she pressed me against her heaving bosom.

"Are you angry," I then asked her.

"I never get angry at anything that is natural," she replied. "I'm just worried that you're suffering."

"Oh, I'm suffering terribly."

"Poor friend." She brushed the tangled hair from my forehead. "Not because of me, I hope."

"No—" I answered. "And yet my love for you has turned into a kind of madness. I'm tormented day and night by the thought that I can lose you, perhaps should lose you."

"But you don't even possess me as yet," said Wanda, with those same moist, quivering, consuming eyes that had already once swept me away. Then she stood up, and her small, translucent hands placed a wreath of blue anemones on the white curly hair of Venus. Half reluctantly I put my arm around Wanda's waist.

"I can't live without you anymore, you beautiful woman," I said. "Believe me, just this once believe me. It's no claptrap, no fantasy. I feel deep in my innermost core that my life is tied to yours. If you leave me, I'll perish, I'll wither away."

"That won't be necessary, for I love you." She took hold of my chin. "Silly!"

"But you're willing to be mine only under certain conditions, while I belong to you unconditionally—"

"That's not wise, Severin," she replied, almost startled. "Don't you know me yet, don't you even want to know me? I am good if I am treated earnestly and reasonably. But if one submits to me too deeply, then I become arrogant—"

"Then be that! Be arrogant, be despotic," I cried in utter exaltation, "only be mine, be mine forever." I lay at her feet, with my arms around her knees.

"This won't end well, my friend," she said earnestly, without stirring.

"Oh, but it should never end!" I cried excitedly, intensely. "Only death should separate us. If you can't be mine, all mine and forever, then *I want to be your slave*, serve you, tolerate anything from you—only just don't push me away."

"Pull yourself together," she said, leaning over and kissing my forehead. "I'm very fond of you, but that's not the way to conquer me, to hold on to me."

"I'm willing to do anything, anything you like—I just don't want to lose you," I cried. "Just not that—I can't stand the thought of it!"

"Stand up."

I obeyed.

"You are truly a strange person," Wanda went on. "So you want to possess me at any price?

"Yes, at any price."

"But what good would it do you to possess me—?" she mused—there was something lurking, something sinister in her eyes—"if I stopped loving you, if I belonged to someone else?"

Cold shivers ran down my spine. I looked at her: she stood before me, so solid and self-assured, and her eyes had a cold glint.

"You see," she said. "You are terrified at the very thought." Suddenly her face beamed with a charming smile.

"Yes, I'm horrified when I vividly imagine that a woman whom I love, who has requited my love, could give herself to another man without showing me the slightest compassion. But do I have a choice? If I love that woman, love her madly, should I proudly turn my back on her and let my boastful strength destroy me? Should I blow my brains out? I have two female ideals. If I can't find my noble, sunny ideal, a kind and faithful woman to share my life, then I won't put up with anything halfway, anything lukewarm! I would rather submit to a woman with no virtue, no fidelity, no compassion. Such a woman in her selfish grandeur is also an ideal. If I can't enjoy the full and total happiness of love, then I want to drain its torments, its tortures to the dregs; then I want the woman I love to mistreat me, betray me, and the more cruelly the better. That too is a pleasure."

"Are you insane?" cried Wanda.

"I love you with all my soul," I continued, "with all my senses, and so deeply that your nearness, your atmosphere are indispensable to me if I am to go on living. So choose between my ideals, Madam. Make of me what you will, your husband or your slave."

"Very good," said Wanda, knitting her small but vividly curving eyebrows. "I find this highly amusing: to utterly control a man who interests me, who loves me. At least I won't lack for entertainment. You were imprudent enough to leave the choice up to me. This is my choice: I want you to be my slave! I am going to turn you into my plaything!"

"Oh! Do that!" I cried, half quaking, half delighted. "If a marriage can be based only on equality, on compatibility, then the greatest passions, by contrast, arise from opposites. We are such opposites, almost hostile to each other. That explains this love of mine, which is part hatred, part fear. In such a relationship, only one person can be the hammer, the other the anvil. I want to be the anvil. I can't be happy if I look down on my beloved. I want to be able to worship a woman, and I can do so only if she is cruel to me."

"But, Severin," Wanda retorted almost angrily, "do you think

I'm capable of mistreating a man who loves me as much as you do and whom I love?"

"Why not, if that makes me worship you all the more? *We can truly love only what stands above us*, a woman who subjugates us through beauty, temperament, intellect, willpower, a woman who becomes our despot."

"So you are attracted to what other people are repulsed by?"

"That's it. That's what's so bizarre about me."

"Well, ultimately there is nothing so distinctive or singular about all your passions, for who doesn't like a beautiful fur, and everyone knows and feels the close kinship between voluptuousness and cruelty."

"But with me, all this is intensified to the highest degree," I replied.

"That means rationality has little power over you, and you are soft, yielding, and sensual by nature."

"Were the martyrs also soft and sensual by nature?"

"The martyrs?"

"Quite the contrary: They were *suprasensual people*, who found joy in suffering, who sought the most dreadful agonies, even death, the way others seek pleasure. And that is the kind of person that I am, Madam: *suprasensual*."

"Just make sure you don't become a martyr out of love, a *martyr to a woman*."

We were sitting on Wanda's small balcony in the warm, fragrant summer night, a twofold roof above us: first the green ceiling of vines, then the canopy of the sky, which was sown with countless stars. From the park came a soft and plaintive caterwauling, and I was perched on a footstool at the feet of my Goddess, talking about my childhood.

"And by then all these singular tendencies had already crystallized in you?" asked Wanda.

"Yes indeed. I can't remember ever not having them. Even in my cradle, as my mother subsequently told me, I was *suprasensual*. I rejected the healthy breasts of the wet nurse, and they had to feed me goat's milk. When I was a little boy, I had an enig-matic fear of women, but that was actually an intense interest in them. I was frightened by the gray vault, the penumbra of a church, and I panicked before the glittering altars and images of saints. On the other hand, I would secretly steal over—as if to a forbidden joy—to a plaster Venus that stood in my father's small library. I would kneel down and recite to her the prayers that had been inculcated in me, the Lord's Prayer, the Hail Mary, and the Credo.

"One night I left my bed in order to visit her. The sickle moon illuminated the way and shed a cold, wan, blue light on the God-dess. I threw myself down before her and kissed her cold feet as I had seen our farmers do when they kissed the feet of the dead Savior.

"I was seized with an uncontrollable yearning.

"I rose and embraced the beautiful cold body and kissed the cold lips. Now I was overcome by a profound terror and I fled. And in my dreams the Goddess stood in front of my bed and threatened me with her raised arm.

"I was sent to school at an early age, and so I shortly began Gymnasium, where I passionately seized upon everything that the ancient world promised to reveal to me. I was soon more fa-miliar with the gods of Greece than with the religion of Jesus. To-gether with Paris I gave Venus the fateful apple, I saw Troy burn, and I followed Odysseus on his wanderings. The primal images of all beautiful things sank deep into my soul, and so at a time when other boys act crude and obscene, I displayed an insupera-ble abhorrence for all that was vile, common, and unsightly.

"And the thing that struck the maturing adolescent as particu-larly vile and unsightly was the love for women as it was first shown to him in its full vulgarity. I avoided any contact with the fair sex—in short, I was insanely suprasensual.

"When I was about fourteen, my mother hired a charming chambermaid, young, pretty, with a curvaceous figure. One day, while I was studying my Tacitus and enthusing about the virtues of the ancient Germanic tribes, the maid was sweeping my room.

Suddenly she stopped, leaned toward me, broom in hand, and two full, fresh, delicious lips touched mine. The kiss of the amorous little cat sent shivers up and down my spine, but I brandished my *Germania* like a shield against the seductress and indignantly stormed out of the room."

Wanda burst into loud laughter. "You are truly one of a kind, but do go on."

"Another episode from that period is unforgettable," I continued. "Countess Sobol, a distant aunt of mine, was visiting my parents. She was a beautiful, majestic woman with a charming smile; but I hated her, for the family regarded her as a Messalina, and my behavior toward her was as bad, nasty, and awkward as could be.

"One day my parents went to the district seat. My aunt decided to make use of their absence and take me to task. Unexpectedly she entered in her fur-lined kazabaika, followed by the cook, the kitchen maid, and the little cat that I had spurned. Wasting no time, they grabbed me and, overcoming my violent resistance, they bound me hand and foot. Next, with a wicked smile my aunt rolled up her sleeves and began laying into me with a heavy switch. She hit me so hard that she drew blood, and for all my heroic valor I finally screamed and wept and begged for mercy. She then had me untied, but I was forced to kneel down, thank her for the punishment, and kiss her hand.

"Now just look at the suprasensual fool! The switch held by the beautiful, voluptuous woman, who looked like an angry monarch in her fur jacket, first aroused my desire for women, and from then on my aunt seemed like the most attractive woman on God's earth.

"My Catonian severity, my timidity with women, were simply nothing but the most sublime sense of beauty; sensuality now became a sort of culture in my imagination, and I swore not to squander its holy sensations on an ordinary creature but to save them for an ideal woman—if possible, the Goddess of Love herself.

"I was very young when I began studying at the university in the capital, where my aunt resided. My room resembled that of

Dr. Faustus. Everything was cluttered and chaotic: towering shelves crammed with books I had gotten dirt-cheap after haggling with a Jewish dealer in Zarvanica, globes, atlases, phials, celestial charts, skulls, animal skeletons, busts of great men. At any moment Mephistopheles as an itinerant Scholastic might have stepped forth from behind the large green stove.

"I studied everything higgledy-piggledy, unsystematically, promiscuously: chemistry, alchemy, literature, astronomy, philosophy, law, anatomy, and history. I read Homer, Virgil, Ossian, Schiller, Goethe, Shakespeare, Cervantes, Voltaire, Molière, the Koran, the Cosmos, Casanova's memoirs. I grew more and more confused, eccentric, and suprasensual every day. In my mind I always pictured a beautiful female ideal; and now and then, amid my skeletons and my leather-bound tomes, she would appear like a vision, reclining on roses, surrounded by cupids. Sometimes she wore Olympian attire and had the severe white face of the plaster Venus, sometimes she had the voluptuous brown braids, the laughing blue eyes, and the ermine-trimmed, red velvet kazabaika of my beautiful aunt.

"One morning, when she again emerged in full, laughing grace from the golden mists of my imagination, I went to see Countess Sobol, who gave me a friendly, indeed hearty welcome, receiving me with a kiss that made all my senses reel. She must have been close to forty by now, but like most of those die-hard demimondaines she was still desirable. She always wore a fur-lined jacket, this one in green velvet with brown stone marten; but none of the severity that had once delighted me was discernible in her.

"Quite the contrary: she felt so little cruelty toward me that without further ado she gave me permission to worship her.

"She had all too soon discovered my suprasensual foolishness and innocence and she enjoyed making me happy. And I—I was truly as blissful as a young god. What pleasure it was for me to kneel down and be allowed to kiss her hands, which had once chastised me. Ah! What wonderful hands! So beautifully shaped, so fine and full and white, and with such darling dimples! I was actually in love only with those hands. I played with them, let them rise and sink in the dark fur, I held them up against a flame and could not see enough of them."

Wanda involuntarily looked at her hands. I noticed it and couldn't help smiling.

"You can tell from the following facts how greatly dominated I was by the suprasensual: in regard to my aunt, I was in love only with the cruel switching I had received from her; and in regard to a young actress I courted some two years later, I was in love only with her roles. I next had a crush on a very respectable lady who feigned an unapproachable virtue but eventually betrayed me with a wealthy Jew. You see: because I was deceived and made a fool of by a woman who shammed the most rigorous principles, the most ideal feelings, I now ardently hate those kinds of poetic and sentimental virtues. Give me a woman who's honest enough to tell me: 'I'm a Pompadour, a Lucretia Borgia,' and I'll worship her."

Wanda stood up and opened the window.

"You have a peculiar way of inflaming the imagination, exciting all nerves, making the pulse beat faster. You provide vice with an aureole so long as it's honest. Your ideal is a bold and brilliant courtesan. Oh, you're the kind of man who can thoroughly corrupt a woman!"

In the middle of the night there was a knock on my pane. I got up, opened the window, and recoiled. There stood Venus in furs, just as she had appeared to me the first time.

"Your stories aroused me," she said, "I'm tossing and turning and I can't sleep. Come and just keep me company."

"Right away."

When I entered her room, Wanda was huddling at the hearth, where she had fanned up a small fire.

"Autumn is setting in," she began, "the nights are already quite cold. I'm afraid it may displease you, but I can't toss off my fur until the room is warm enough."

"Displease—you scamp! . . . You do know, Madam . . ." I threw my arm around her and kissed her.

"Of course I know, but how did you develop this passion for fur?"

"It's innate," I answered. "I already showed it as a child. Incidentally, fur excites all high-strung people—an effect that is consistent with both universal and natural laws. It is a physical stimulus, which is just as strangely tingling and which no one can entirely resist. Science has recently demonstrated a kinship between electricity and warmth—in any case, their effects on the human organism are related. The tropics produce more passionate people, a heated atmosphere causes excitement. The same holds for electricity. Hence the bewitchingly beneficial influence that *cats* exert on highly sensitive and intelligent people; this has made these long-tailed graces of the animal kingdom, these sweet, spark-spraying electric batteries the darlings of a Mohammed, a Cardinal Richelieu, a Crébillon, a Rousseau, or a Wieland."

"So a woman wearing fur," cried Wanda, "is nothing but a big cat, a charged electric battery?"

"Certainly," I replied, "and that's how I account for the symbolic meaning that fur took on as an attribute of power and beauty. It was in those terms that earlier monarchs and ruling aristocracies laid exclusive claim to fur in their clothing hierarchies, and great painters laid exclusive claim to it for the queens of beauty. Thus Raphael found no more delightful frame than fur for the divine curves of Fornarina, and Titian for the rosy body of his beloved."

"Thank you for the learned erotic treatise," said Wanda, "but you haven't told me everything. You associate something very singular with fur."

"Indeed I do," I cried. "I've already told you repeatedly that suffering has a strange appeal for me, that nothing can so readily fan my passion as the tyranny, the cruelty, and, above all, the infidelity of a beautiful woman. Nor can I imagine her without fur—this woman, this strange ideal derived from the aesthetics of ugliness: a Nero's soul in a Phryne's body."

"I understand," Wanda threw in. "There's something domineering, imposing about a woman in fur."

"It's not just that," I went on. "You know, Madam, that I'm 'suprasensual,' that everything is rooted more in my imagination and nourished by it. I was precocious and overwrought when I got hold of *The Legends of the Martyrs* at the age of ten. I remember reading with a horror that was actually delight: the way the martyrs languished in dungeons, were roasted on grills, were shot through by arrows, boiled in pitch, thrown to wild beasts, nailed to crosses, and they suffered the most dreadful fates with something like joy. From then on, agony, gruesome torture seemed like a pleasure, especially when inflicted by a beautiful woman, since for me all that was poetic and demonic had always been concentrated in women. Indeed I practiced a downright cult.

"I saw sensuality as sacred, indeed the only sacredness, I saw woman and her beauty as divine since her calling is the most important task of existence: the propagation of the species. I saw woman as the personification of nature, as *Isis*, and man as her priest, her slave; and I pictured her treating him as cruelly as Nature, who, when she no longer needs something that has served her, tosses it away, while her abuse, indeed her killing it, are its lascivious bliss.

"I envied King Gunther whom powerful Brunhilde tied up on their wedding night; the poor troubadour whom his capricious mistress sewed up in wolf skins and then hunted like a wild prey. I envied Sir Ctirad, whom Sharka the bold Amazon cunningly snared in the forest near Prague, dragged back to Castle Divin, and then, after whiling away some time with him, she had him broken on the wheel—"

"Disgusting!" cried Wanda. "I only wish you would fall into the hands of a member of that savage sisterhood. The poetry would vanish once you were in a wolf skin, under the teeth of hounds, or on the wheel."

"Do you believe that? I don't."

"You've taken leave of your senses. You're really not very bright."

"Perhaps. But let me go on. I greedily devoured stories about the most abominable cruelties and I especially loved pictures, engravings that showed them. And I saw all the bloody tyrants who

ever sat on a throne, the inquisitors who tortured, roasted, slaugh-
tered the heretics, all those women whom the pages of history
have depicted as lascivious, beautiful, and violent, such as Libussa,
Lucretia Borgia, Agnes of Hungary, Queen Margot, Isabeau, Sul-
tana Roxolane, the Russian tsarinas of the eighteenth century—I
saw them all in furs or in robes trimmed with ermine."

"And so now fur arouses your bizarre fantasies," cried Wanda,
and she began coquettishly draping herself in her splendid fur
mantle, so that the dark, shiny sables flashed delightfully around
her breasts, her arms. "Well, how do you feel now? Are you already half broken on the wheel?"

Her green, piercing eyes rested on me with a strange, scornful
relish as I, overcome with passion, threw myself down before her
and flung my arms around her.

"Yes—you've aroused my most cherished fantasy," I cried,
"which has been dormant long enough."

"And that would be?" She placed her hand on the back of my
neck.

Under that small, warm hand, under her gaze, which fell upon
me, tenderly inquisitive, through half-closed eyelids, I was seized
with a sweet intoxication.

"*To be the slave of a woman, a beautiful woman, whom I
love, whom I worship—!*"

"And who mistreats you for it," Wanda broke in, laughing.

"Yes, who ties me up and whips me, who kicks me when she
belongs to another man."

"And who, after driving you insane with jealousy and forcing
you to face your successful rival, goes so far in her exuberance
that she turns you over to him and abandons you to his brutality.
Why not? Do you like the final tableau any less?"

I gave Wanda a terrified look. "You're exceeding my dreams."

"Yes, we women are inventive," she said. "Be careful. When
you find your ideal, she might easily treat you more cruelly than
you like."

"I'm afraid I've already found my ideal!" I cried and pressed
my hot face into her lap.

"Not me certainly?" cried Wanda, hurling away the fur, striding about the room, and laughing. She was still laughing as I went downstairs; and while I stood musing in the courtyard, I could still hear her malevolent and hilarious laughter.

"So should I embody your ideal?" said Wanda roguishly when we met in the park.

At first I was at a loss to answer. The most contradictory emotions struggled inside me. Meanwhile she sat down on one of the stone benches and played with a flower.

"Well—should I?"

I knelt and clutched her hands.

"I beg you once again: Be my wife, my faithful, honest spouse. If you can't do that, then be my ideal, and fully, without restraint, without qualification."

"You know that I will give you my hand in a year's time if you are the man I am looking for," Wanda countered very earnestly. "But I believe you will be more grateful to me if I make your fantasies come true. Well, which do you prefer?"

"I believe that everything lurking in my imagination is in your nature too."

"You are mistaken."

"I believe," I went on, "that you enjoy having a man entirely in your control, torturing—"

"No, no," she cried briskly. "Or maybe so." She pondered. "I don't understand myself anymore," she continued, "but I must confess something. You've corrupted my imagination, inflamed my blood. I'm starting to enjoy all those things. Your enthusiasm when you talk about a Pompadour, a Catherine the Great, and all the other selfish, frivolous, and cruel women is entrancing. It sinks into my soul and drives me to emulate those women, who, despite all their evil, were slavishly worshiped during their lifetimes and still work miracles from the grave.

"In the end you'll turn me into a miniature female despot, a Pompadour for domestic use."

"Well, Madam," I said ebulliently, "if that's in you, then yield to your natural tendency, but don't go halfway. If you can't be a decent, faithful wife, then be a devil."

I was exhausted, excited, the closeness of the beautiful woman seized hold of me like a fever. I no longer know what I said, but I do recall that I kissed her feet and finally picked up her foot and placed it on the nape of my neck. But she swiftly pulled it back and stood up almost angrily. "If you love me, Severin"— she spoke quickly, her voice sharp and imperious, "then never talk about those things again. Do you understand? Never again. Otherwise I could really—" She smiled and sat back down.

"I'm utterly serious," I cried, half raving. "I worship you so much that I am willing to tolerate anything from you as the price for being near you for the rest of my life."

"Severin, I warn you again."

"Your warning is useless. Do what you like with me, but don't push me entirely away."

"Severin," Wanda retorted, "I'm a young, frivolous woman. It's dangerous for you to submit to me so completely. You'll actually wind up as my plaything. Who will protect you if I abuse your insanity?"

"Your noble character will protect me."

"Power corrupts."

"Then be corrupt," I cried, "kick me."

Wanda slung her arms around my neck, peered into my eyes, and shook her head. "I'm afraid I won't be able to, but I'll try it for your sake, because I love you, Severin, as I have loved no other man."

The next day she suddenly took her hat and her scarf and had me accompany her to the bazaar. There she looked at whips, long whips with short handles, the kind used on dogs.

"These should do the job," said the vendor.

"No, they're much too small," replied Wanda, casting a side-long glance at me. "I need a big—"

"For a bulldog no doubt?" asked the merchant.

"Yes," she cried, "the sort of whip that was used on rebellious slaves in Russia."

She searched and finally selected a whip the sight of which left me somewhat queasy.

"Well, goodbye, Severin," she said, "I have to do some more shopping, and you can't accompany me."

I said goodbye and went strolling. On the way back, I saw Wanda emerging from a furrier's shop. She beckoned to me.

"Give it some further thought," she began delightedly, "I've never made a secret of the fact that I was captivated chiefly by your earnest, pensive character. Now it does intrigue me to see this earnest man at my feet, completely devoted, downright enraptured—but will this intrigue last? A woman loves a man, but she mistreats a slave and ultimately kicks him away."

"Well, then kick me away when you're fed up with me," I retorted. "I want to be your slave."

"I realize that dangerous faculties lie dormant in me," said Wanda after we walked a few steps. "You're awakening them and not to your advantage. You know how to depict pleasure, cruelty, and wantonness in such tempting colors—what would you say if I tried my hand at it and started with you, like the tyrant Dionysius, who broiled the inventor of the iron bull in his own invention in order to see whether his wailing, his death rattle actually sounded like the bellowing of a bull. Might I be a female Dionysius?"

"Be one," I cried. "Then my fantasy will be fulfilled. I belong to you for better or for worse—the choice is yours. I'm driven by the destiny that's in my heart—demonic . . . overpowering."

My darling!

I do not wish to see you today or tomorrow—not until the evening of the following day, and at that point I want to see you as my slave.

Your Mistress,
Wanda

"As my slave" was underlined. I reread the note, which I received early in the morning. Then I had a donkey saddled—the right animal for a scholar—and rode off to the mountains, hop-

ing to numb my passion, my yearning in the magnificent nature
of the Carpathians.

I was back again—tired, hungry, thirsty, and, above all, in love. I
quickly changed clothes and knocked on her door several moments later.

"Come in!"

I entered. She stood in the middle of the room, wearing a
white satin robe that flowed down her body like light, and
a scarlet satin kazabaika with a rich, luxuriant ermine trimming.
In her powdered snowy hair there was a small diamond tiara,
her arms were crossed on her bosom, her eyebrows were
knitted.

Wanda!" I hurried toward her, tried to throw my arm around
her, to kiss her. She took a step back and scrutinized me from top
to bottom.

"Slave!"

"Mistress!" I knelt down and kissed the hem of her robe.

"That's the ticket."

"Oh, how beautiful you are!"

"Do you like me?" She went to the mirror and viewed herself
with proud delight.

"I'm going insane!"

Her lower lip twitched scornfully, and she gave me a mocking
glance through half-closed eyelids.

"Give me the whip."

I peered around the room.

"No," she cried, "just keep kneeling!" She stepped over to the
fireplace, took the whip from the mantelpiece, and, smirking at
me, she made the whip whistle through the air. Then she slowly
tucked up one sleeve of her fur jacket.

"Wonderful woman!" I cried.

"Silence, slave!" She suddenly glared, indeed wildly, and
struck me with the whip. A second later, however, she tenderly
put her arm around my neck and leaned compassionately toward
me. "Did I hurt you?" she asked, half embarrassed, half anxious.

"No!" I retorted. "And even if you had, pain that you inflict on me is pleasure. Just whip away if you enjoy it."

"But I don't enjoy it."

Again I was seized with that bizarre intoxication. "Whip me!" I begged. "Whip me ruthlessly!"

Wanda swung the whip and struck me twice. "Is that enough now?"

"No."

"Seriously, no?"

"Whip me, please, it's a pleasure."

"Yes, because you know very well that it's not serious," she replied. "You know I don't have the heart to hurt you. I'm repelled by the whole business. If I were really the kind of woman who whips her slaves, you'd be horrified."

"No, Wanda," I said, "I love you more than myself, I'm devoted to you in life and in death. You can seriously do anything you please to me—whatever your wantonness suggests."

"Severin!"

"Kick me!" I cried and threw myself down in front of her, my face on the floor.

"I hate all playacting," said Wanda impatiently.

"Well, then abuse me seriously."

A sinister pause.

"Severin, this is my last warning," Wanda began.

"If you love me, then be cruel to me," I pleaded, peeking up at her.

"If I love you?" Wanda repeated. "Very well, then!" She stepped back and contemplated me with a dark smirk. "*Well, then be my slave and feel what it means to be put in a woman's hands.*" That same moment she kicked me.

"So, how do you like that, slave?"

Then she swung the whip.

"Straighten up!"

I tried to stand. "Not like that," she commanded. "On your knees."

I obeyed and she began whipping me.

The strokes fell swiftly and forcefully on my back, my arms. Each blow cut into my flesh and continued burning there, but the pains delighted me, for they came from the woman whom I worshiped, for whom I was ready at any moment to lay down my life.

Now she stopped. "I'm beginning to enjoy it," she said. "That's enough for today, but I'm devilishly curious to measure the extent of your strength. I feel a cruel lust to see you quaking and writhing under my whip, and finally to hear you moaning, wailing, on and on, until you beg for mercy, and I ruthlessly keep whipping until you faint. You've aroused dangerous forces in my character. But now, stand up."

I grabbed her hand to press my lips upon it.

"What impudence!"

She kicked me away.

"Out of my sight, slave!"

After a night of confused and feverish dreams, I woke up. It was barely dawn.

What was true among the things drifting through my memory? What had I experienced and what had I merely dreamed? I had been whipped—that much was certain; I could still feel every single stroke, I could count the red, burning welts on my body. And *she* had whipped me. Yes, now I knew everything.

My fantasy had come true. How did I feel? Was I disappointed by the reality of my dream?

No, I was just somewhat tired, but her cruelty filled me with delight. Oh, how I loved her, how I worshiped her! Ah, none of this even remotely expresses what I felt for her, how thoroughly devoted I was to her. What bliss to be her slave!

She called from the balcony. I hurried up the steps. There she stood on the threshold, amiably offering me her hand. "I'm ashamed," she said, while I hugged her, and she buried her head on my chest.

"What?"

"Try to forget yesterday's ugly scene," she said in a quivering voice. "I made your insane fantasy come true. Now let's be reasonable and happy and love one another, and in a year's time I'll be your wife."

"My Mistress," I cried, "and I your slave!"

"Not another word about slavery, about cruelty or the whip," Wanda broke in. "The only favor I'll still do for you is to wear the fur jacket. Come and help me into it."

The small bronze clock, topped by a Cupid who had just shot his arrow, struck midnight.

I stood up, I wanted to get out.

Wanda said nothing, but she embraced me and pulled me back to the sofa and began to kiss me again, and there was something so intelligible, so convincing about that mute language—

And it said even more than I dared to grasp. Such a yearning devotion imbued Wanda's entire being, and what voluptuous softness lay in her half-closed, twilight eyes, in the red flood of her hair shimmering lightly under the white powder, in the white and red satin that rustled around her at every movement, the swelling ermine of the kazabaika, in which she casually nestled.

"I beg you," I stammered, "but you'll be angry."

"Do whatever you like with me," she whispered.

"Well, kick me, I beg you. Otherwise I'll go crazy!"

"Haven't I forbidden you?" Wanda snapped. "You're incorrigible."

"Ah, I'm so dreadfully in love." I had knelt down and was pressing my hot face into her lap.

"I truly believe," said Wanda, musing, "that your entire madness is simply a demonic, unsated sensuality. *Our unnaturalness must create such diseases*. If you were less virtuous, you'd be completely sensible."

"Well, then smarten me up," I murmured. My hands wallowed in her hair and in the shimmering fur, which heaved and sank on her surging bosom like a moonlit wave, confusing all my senses.

And I kissed her—no, she kissed me, so wildly, so ruthlessly, as if to kill me with her kisses. I was delirious, I had long since lost my powers of reasoning, and now I couldn't breathe anymore. I tried to extricate myself.

"What's wrong?" asked Wanda.

"I'm suffering terribly."

"Suffering?" She burst into loud, wicked laughter.

"Laugh all you like!" I moaned. "Don't you have an inkling—?"

She suddenly turned very serious, drew my head up in her hands, and vehemently pulled me to her breasts.

"Wanda!" I stammered.

"Of course. You enjoy suffering," she said, and began laughing again. "But just wait, I'll make you reasonable soon enough."

"No, I don't want to ask any more questions," I cried. "Whether you belong to me forever or only for a blissful instant, I want to enjoy my happiness. You're mine now, and it's better to lose you than never to possess you."

"Now you're being reasonable," she said, and kissed me again with her murderous lips, and I tore apart the ermine, the lace covering, and her bare breasts surged against my chest.

Then I fainted. . . .

The first thing I recall is the moment when I saw blood dripping from my hand and I apathetically asked: "Did you scratch me?"

"No, I think I bit you."

It's truly strange how every relationship in life takes on a different cast as soon as a new person enters.

We spent marvelous days with each other, we visited the mountains, the lakes, we read together, and I finished my portrait of Wanda.

And how we loved each other, how radiant was her charming face.

Then along came a friend of hers, a divorcée, somewhat older, somewhat more experienced, and somewhat less scrupulous than Wanda, and her experience was brought to bear in every respect.

Wanda frowned and acted somewhat impatient toward me. Had she stopped loving me?

For almost two weeks that unbearable constraint. Her friend was staying with her, we were never alone. A circle of gentlemen surrounded the two young women. With my earnestness, my melancholy, I played a foolish role as a lover. Wanda treated me like a stranger.

One day, during a stroll, she lagged behind with me. I saw that it was intentional and I rejoiced. What did she say?

"My friend doesn't understand how I can love you. She finds you neither handsome nor particularly appealing, and then she entertains me from morning till late at night, talking about the glamorous, frivolous life in the capital. She tells me about the advantages I could demand, the wonderful matches I would find, the handsome and noble suitors I'd be bound to captivate. But what good is all that? It's you I love."

For an instant I couldn't breathe. Then I said: "I absolutely don't want to stand in the way of your happiness, Wanda. Don't show me any further consideration." I doffed my hat and let her go ahead. She gaped at me, astonished, but didn't say a word.

However, when I happened to get near her on the way back, she stealthily squeezed my hand, and her gaze was so warm, so auspicious, that all the torments of these days were promptly forgotten, all wounds were healed.

Now I again knew so clearly how much I loved her.

"My friend has complained about you," Wanda told me.

"She may sense that I despise her."

"Why do you despise her, you little fool?" cried Wanda, grabbing my ears with both hands.

"Because she's a hypocrite," I said. "I can respect a woman only if she is truly virtuous or openly lives for pleasure."

"Like me," Wanda countered jokingly. "But look, my child, a woman can do so only in the rarest cases. She can be neither as cheerfully sensual nor as spiritually free as a man. Her love is al-

ways a blend of sensuality and spiritual attachment. Her heart
longs to captivate the man permanently, while she herself is prey
to change. And so, usually against her will, a dichotomy, a pack
of lies and deception comes into her conduct, into her being, and
corrupts her character."

"That's certainly true," I said. "The transcendental character
that a woman wants to force upon her love will lead her to
cheat—"

"But the world demands it," Wanda broke in. "Just look at
this woman. In Lemberg she has her husband and her lover and
here she's found a new admirer, and she deceives all three of
them and yet she's adored by this trio and esteemed by the
world."

"Fine with me," I cried. "But she simply ought to leave you
out of the game. Why, she treats you like a commodity."

"Why not," the beautiful woman briskly interrupted me.
"Every woman has the instinct, the propensity to profit from her
charms, and there's a lot to be said for giving oneself without
love, without pleasure. While doing so, a woman remains quite
cold-blooded and can gain her advantage."

"Wanda, do you mean that?"

"Why not?" she responded. "Make a point of remembering
what I'm about to tell you: *Never feel safe with the woman you
love,* for a woman's nature conceals more dangers that you think.
Women are neither as *good* as their admirers and defenders
would have it nor as *bad* as their enemies make them out to be. *A
woman's character is her lack of character.* The best woman sinks
momentarily into filth, the worst woman rises unexpectedly to
great good deeds, putting her despisers to shame. No woman is
so good or so evil as not to be capable at any moment of both the
most diabolical and most divine, both the foulest and the purest
thoughts, feelings, actions. Despite all progress of civilization,
women have remained exactly as they emerged from the hand of
Nature. A woman has the character of a *savage,* who acts loyal
or disloyal, generous or gruesome, depending on whatever impulse happens to rule him at the moment. In all times, only deep

and earnest formation has created the moral character. Thus, a man, no matter how selfish, how malevolent he may be, always follows *principles,* while a woman always follows only *impulses.* Never forget this and never feel safe with the woman you love."

Her friend had departed. Finally an evening alone with Wanda. It was as if after withdrawing her love, she had been saving all of it for this one blissful evening—she was so kind, so intimate, so full of grace.

What bliss to cling to her lips, to die away in her arms—and then she rested on my chest, so utterly relaxed, so utterly devoted to me, and our gazes, so drunk with bliss, submerged in one another.

I still could not believe, could not grasp that this woman was mine, all mine.

"She's right about one thing," Wanda began without stirring, without even opening her eyes, as if asleep.

"Who?"

She was silent.

"Your friend?"

She nodded. "Yes, she's right. You're not a man, you're a dreamer, a charming admirer, and you'd certainly make an invaluable slave, but I can't picture you as a husband."

I recoiled.

"What's wrong? You're trembling."

"I'm terrified at the thought of losing you so easily," I replied.

"Well, are you any less happy for it?" she countered. "Does it deprive you of any of your joys to know that I belonged to other men before you, that others will possess me after you, and would you have less pleasure if someone else were happy at the same time as you?"

"Wanda!"

"Look," she said, "that would be a solution. You never want to lose me, I care for you, and spiritually you're so attractive that I would like to live with you forever if along with you—"

"What a dreadful idea!" I yelled. "You horrify me."

"And do you love me any the less?"

"Quite the opposite."

Wanda was now leaning on her left arm. "I think," she said, "that if a woman wants to captivate a man forever she must, above all, be unfaithful to him. What decent woman has ever been so greatly worshiped as a hetaera?"

"A woman's infidelity is certainly a painful stimulus, the supreme voluptuousness."

"For you too?" Wanda asked quickly.

"For me too."

"And what if I provided you with this pleasure?" Wanda taunted.

"Then I will suffer dreadfully, yet worship you all the more," I replied. "But you must never deceive me, you must have the demonic greatness to tell me: 'I will love only you, but I will make anyone who appeals to me happy.'"

Wanda shook her head: "I abhor deception. I'm an honest person—but what man doesn't succumb under the brunt of truth? If I told you, 'This sensually cheerful life, this paganism are my ideal,' would you have the strength to endure it?"

"Certainly. I'm willing to endure anything from you so long as I don't lose you. I can feel how little I mean to you."

"But Severin—"

"It's true," I said, "and that's precisely why—"

"Why you'd like. . . ." She smirked roguishly. "Have I guessed it?"

"To be your slave!" I cried. "With no will of my own! To be your absolute property, with which you can do as you please and which can therefore never be a burden on you. While you drink life to the full amid sumptuous luxury, while you enjoy cheerful happiness, Olympian love, I would like to serve you, put your shoes on your feet and take them off."

"You're really not all that wrong," replied Wanda, "for only as my slave could you endure my loving others. And besides, the freedom of enjoyment in the ancient world is unthinkable without slavery. Oh, a person must feel like a God when he sees others kneeling before him, trembling. I want to have slaves, do you hear, Severin?"

"Am I not your slave?"

"Now listen," said Wanda excitedly, grabbing my hand. "I want to be yours so long as I love you."

"One month?"

"Perhaps even two."

"And then?"

"Then you'll be my slave."

"And you?"

"I? Why do you ask? I am a Goddess and sometimes I descend quietly to you, very quietly and secretly from my Olympus.

"But what is all this about?" said Wanda, propping her head on her hands, gazing into the distance. "A golden fantasy that can never come true." A brutal, sinister melancholy infused her entire being. I had never seen her like this.

"And why can't it materialize?" I began.

"Because slavery doesn't exist in our country."

"Then let's go to a country where it still exists, to the Orient, to Turkey," I said eagerly.

"You'd want to—Severin—seriously," retorted Wanda. Her eyes were burning.

"Yes, I seriously want to be your slave," I went on. "I want your power over me to be sanctified by law, I want my life to be in your hands, I want nothing in this world to be able to protect me or save me from you. Oh, what voluptuousness to feel dependent entirely on your whim, your mood, a flick of your finger! And then what bliss when you feel merciful for a change and allow the slave to kiss the lips to which he clings for life or death!" I knelt and leaned my hot forehead on her lap.

"You're feverish, Severin," said Wanda, excited, "and do you really love me so endlessly?" She hugged me and covered me with kisses.

"So you want to?" she began, hesitant.

"I swear to you here, by God and my honor, that I am your

slave wherever and whenever you like, as soon as you order me,"
I cried, barely in control of myself.

"And if I take you at your word?" asked Wanda.

"Do it."

"It's the most appealing thing in the world," she said, "to find
a man who worships me, and whom I love with all my soul, and
to know that he's so utterly devoted to me and dependent on my
will, my whim, and to possess that man as a slave, while I—"

She eyed me strangely.

"If I become quite frivolous, then it's your fault," she continued. "I almost believe you're already afraid of me, but I have
your oath."

"And I will keep it."

"I'll make sure of that," she retorted. "Now I'm starting to
enjoy it, now it should no longer remain a fantasy, by God. You
will be my slave, and I—I will try to be *Venus in Furs.*"

I had thought I finally knew and understood this woman, but
now I saw that I would have to start all over again. A short time
ago she had been so repelled by my fantasies, and now she was
so seriously acting upon them.

She drew up a contract binding me by my oath and word of
honor to be her slave as long as she desired it.

With her arm slung around my neck, she read the outrageous,
unbelievable document to me; every sentence was sealed with a
kiss.

"But the contract contains only obligations for me," I said,
teasing her.

"Naturally," she retorted very earnestly. "You are no longer
my lover, and that releases me from all obligations, all considera-
tions toward you. You must then view my favor as a grace. You
have no rights and therefore cannot bring any right to bear. My
power over you must be unlimited. Think, you man, you're not
much better than a dog, a lifeless object. You are my thing, my
toy, which I can smash just to while away an hour. You are nothing, and I am everything. Do you understand?"

She laughed and kissed me again, and yet I felt a cold chill running through my body.

"Won't you allow me a few conditions—?" I began.

"Conditions?" She frowned. "Ah, you're already scared or you're having second thoughts. But you're too late, I have your oath, your word of honor. Still, let me hear your conditions."

"First of all, I would like our contract to stipulate that you will never fully leave me and then that you will never subject me to the brutality of any of your admirers—"

"But Severin," cried Wanda in a saddened voice, with tears in her eyes. "You can believe that if a man loves me so deeply, puts himself so entirely in my hands—" She faltered.

"No! No!" I said, covering her hands with kisses. "I fear nothing from you that could dishonor me. Forgive me for that ugly lapse."

Wanda smiled blissfully, put her cheek on mine, and seemed to be musing.

"You've forgotten something," she whispered, now roguishly, "the most important thing."

"A condition?"

"Yes, that I must always appear in fur," cried Wanda. "But this I promise you: I'll wear it simply because it makes me feel like a despot, and I want to be very cruel to you—do you understand?"

"Should I sign the contract?" I asked.

"Not yet," said Wanda. "I want to add your conditions. Besides, you're going to sign it in the right place."

"Constantinople?"

"No. I've thought it over. What good is having a slave where everyone has slaves? I want to be *alone in having a slave* in our educated, sober, Philistine world—a slave with no will of his own, a slave who is put into my hands not by the law, not by my privilege or brutal violence, but solely by the power of my beauty and my being. I find that piquant. At any rate, we're going to a country where nobody knows us, so that you can appear as my servant before the entire world without any ceremony. Perhaps Italy, perhaps Rome or Naples."

We were sitting on Wanda's sofa, she in the ermine jacket, her

loosened hair like a lion's mane down her back, and she clung to
my lips, sucking my soul from my body. My head whirled, my
blood began to seethe, my heart pounded violently against hers.

"I want to be completely in your hands, Wanda," I suddenly
exclaimed in a frenzy of passion, unable to think clearly or make
a free decision. "With no qualification, with no restriction on
your power over me, I want to surrender to your despotism unconditionally." While speaking, I had slipped down from the
couch to her feet and now I gazed up at her euphorically.

"How handsome you are now," she cried. "Your eyes are half
broken as in a trance—they delight me, they sweep me away. If
you were whipped to death, your gaze would have to be wonderful as you breathed your last. You have the eyes of a martyr."

At times I nevertheless felt somewhat queasy about handing myself over to a woman so totally, so unconditionally. What if she
abused my passion, her power?

Well, then I would experience what has occupied my imagination since childhood, always filling me with sweet horror. A
foolish anxiety! It was a mischievous game she was playing with
me, nothing more. She did love me, and she was so good, a noble
nature, incapable of any breach of trust. But it was up to her—
she could if she wished. What charm in that doubt, that fear!

Now I understood Manon Lescaut and the poor chevalier, who
worshiped her even when she was another man's mistress—and
even in the pillory.

Love knows no virtue, no merit; it loves and forgives and tol-
erates everything because it must. We are not guided by reason,
nor do the assets or blemishes that we discover tempt us to devotion or intimidate us. It is a sweet, mournful, mysterious power
that drives us, and we stop thinking, feeling, wishing, we let ourselves drift along and never ask where we are drifting.

A Russian prince appeared on the Promenade for the first time
that day, causing a sensation with his athletic build, his marvelous face, the splendor of his bearing. The women in particular

gaped at him as if at a wild beast, but he strode sullenly along the park walks, heeding no one. He was accompanied by two servants: an African dressed entirely in red satin and a Circassian in full, flashing military garb. Suddenly the Russian spotted Wanda. He riveted his cold, piercing gaze upon her, indeed turned his head toward her; and once she had passed, he remained standing and peered after her.

And she—she simply devoured him with her sparkling green eyes—and did all she could to run into him again.

Her sly coquetry when walking, when moving, when looking at him made my heart bleed. As we were going home, I made a comment about it. She frowned.

"What do you want?" she said. "The prince is a man who could please me, who even dazzles me, and I am free, I can do as I like—"

"Don't you love me anymore?" I stammered in terror.

"I love only you," she retorted, "but I will let the prince court me."

"Wanda!"

"Aren't you my slave?" she said calmly. "Am I not Venus, the cruel Nordic Venus in furs?"

I held my tongue; I literally felt crushed by her words; her cold gaze stabbed my heart like a dagger.

"You will immediately find out the prince's name and address and all his circumstances," she went on, "—do you understand?"

"But—"

"Don't argue! Obey!" cried Wanda with a severity that I would never have thought possible in her. "Do not let me set eyes on you again until you can answer all my questions."

It was not until afternoon that I could bring Wanda the desired information. She had me stand before her like a domestic while she leaned back in the easy chair, listening with a smile. Then she nodded: she appeared satisfied.

"Get me the footstool!" she tersely ordered.

I obeyed, and after I set it in front of her and she put her feet on it, I remained on my knees.

"How will this end?" I asked sadly after a brief pause.

She burst into mischievous laughter. "It hasn't even started."

"You're more heartless than I thought," I replied, offended.

"Severin," Wanda began earnestly. "I've done nothing as yet, not the slightest thing, and you already call me heartless. What will happen when I carry out your fantasies, when I lead a free and merry life, surround myself with a circle of admirers, and, entirely as your ideal, kick you and whip you?"

"You're taking my fantasy too seriously."

"Too seriously? Once I go through with it, I can't just stop with a quip," she countered. "You know how I hate all games, all playacting. You wanted this. Was it my idea or yours? Have I inveigled you or did you inflame my imagination? Now, of course, I'm serious."

"Wanda," I replied lovingly, "please listen to me. We love each other so endlessly, we're so happy—do you want to sacrifice our whole future to a whim?"

"It's no longer a whim!" she cried.

"What is it then?" I asked, terrified.

"It must have been latent in me," she murmured, lost in thought. "Perhaps it would never have seen the light of day, but you awoke it, developed it, and now that it has become a powerful drive, now that it fills me entirely, now that I enjoy it, now that I can't and won't help it—now you want to back out. You—are you a man?"

"Dear, darling Wanda!" I began caressing her, kissing her.

"Leave me alone—you're not a man—"

"And you?" I flared up.

"I'm obstinate," she said, "you know that. I'm not strong in fantasizing and I'm as weak as you in carrying fantasies out. But when I decide on something, I go through with it, and all the more definitely the more resistance I find. Leave me alone!"

She shoved me away and stood up.

"Wanda!" I likewise stood up and faced her eye-to-eye.

"Now you know me," she went on. "I warn you again. You still have the choice. I'm not forcing you to be my slave."

"Wanda," I answered, moved. Tears came to my eyes. "You don't know how much I love you."

Her lips twitched scornfully.

"You're wrong. You're making yourself out to be uglier than you are. Your character is much too good, too noble—"

"What do you know about my character?" she vehemently interrupted me. "You will get to know my true nature."

"Wanda!"

"Decide. Do you want to submit unconditionally?"

"And if I say no?"

"Then . . ."

She stepped toward me, cold and scornful, and as she now stood before me, her arms crossed on her bosom, with that nasty smirk on her lips, she was truly the despotic woman of my fantasies. Her features seemed hard, and there was nothing in her gaze that promised goodness or mercy. "Well . . ." she finally said.

"You're angry," I said, "you're going to whip me."

"Oh, no!" she retorted. "I'm letting you go. You're free. I won't hold you."

"Wanda—me, the man who loves you so much—"

"Yes, you, Sir, who worship me," she cried disdainfully, "but you are a coward, a liar, and not a man of your word. Leave me immediately—"

"Wanda—!"

"Sir!"

The blood rushed to my heart. I prostrated myself at her feet and started crying.

"Tears into the bargain!" she began to laugh. Oh! That laughter was dreadful. "Go away—I never want to see you again."

"My God!" I exclaimed, beside myself. "I want to do everything you command, be your slave, your thing, which you can do with as you like—but don't push me away . . . I'll die—I can't live without you." I threw my arms around her knees and covered her hand with kisses.

"Yes, you must be my slave, feel the whip—for you're not a man," she murmured. And that was what cut me to the quick—the fact that her words were not angry, not even agitated; instead she was fully composed. "Now I know you, you dog, you. You worship when you're kicked and you worship all the more deeply the more you're mistreated. Now I know you, but you're really going to know me."

She strode back and forth while I remained kneeling, crushed, my head hanging, tears running.

"Come to me," Wanda snarled, settling on the sofa. I obeyed and sat at her side. She glared at me; then all at once her eyes virtually lit up from the inside. With a smile she drew me to her bosom and began kissing the tears from my eyes.

That was what was so humorous about my situation: Like the bear in Lili's park, I could flee but didn't want to, and I tolerated everything the instant she threatened to give me my freedom.

If only she had picked up the whip again! There was something eerie about her kind treatment of me. I felt like a small, trapped mouse with which a beautiful cat is daintily playing, ready at any moment to tear it to shreds—and my mouse heart was in danger of bursting.

What was she up to? What did she have in store for me?

She seemed to have completely forgotten about the contract, forgotten about my slavehood. Or was it mere willfulness? Had she given up the entire plan the instant I had stopped resisting, the instant I had bowed to her sovereign whim?

How good she was to me now, how tender, how loving. We spent blissful days together.

Once she had me read aloud the scene between Faust and Mephistopheles, in which the latter appears as an itinerant Scholastic; her eyes hung on me with a strange contentment.

"I don't understand," she said when I was done, "how a man can act out and expound great and beautiful thoughts with such marvelous clarity, acuity, and perception and yet be such a dreamer, a suprasensual Peter Schlemihl."[9]

"So you were satisfied," I said, kissing her hand.

She tenderly stroked my forehead. "I love you, Severin," she whispered. "I don't think I could love any other man. Let's be sensible, all right?"

Rather than answering, I took her in my arms. A deeply intimate, melancholy happiness filled my breast, my eyes moistened, a tear dropped upon her hand.

"How can you cry?!" she exclaimed. "You're a child."

During a pleasure drive we ran into the Russian prince in his carriage. It was obvious that he was unpleasantly surprised to find me at Wanda's side and he seemed to want to drill through me with his gray, electric eyes. But she appeared not to notice him. At that moment I would have preferred to kneel before her and kiss her feet. Her gaze glided indifferently over him as over an inanimate object, say, a tree, and she then turned to me with her gracious smile.

When I said good night to her, she suddenly looked distracted and out of sorts for no reason. What could have been on her mind?

"I'm sorry you're going," she said as I stood on the threshold.

"It's entirely up to you to shorten the period of my testing. Give up torturing me," I pleaded.

"So you don't think that this constraint is a torture for me too," Wanda threw in.

"Then end it," I cried, embracing her. "Be my wife."

"*Never, Severin*," she said gently, but very firmly.

"What do you mean?"

I was terrified to the very core of my soul.

"*You are not the man for me.*"

I looked at her, slowly withdrew my arm from around her waist, and left the room; and she—she didn't call me back.

A sleepless night. I made so many decisions and discarded them again. In the morning I wrote her a letter declaring that our relationship was over. My hand trembled while writing, and when I sealed the letter I burned my fingers.

As I climbed the stairs to hand the letter to the chambermaid, my knees were buckling.

Now the door opened, and Wanda stuck out her head, which was covered with curlers.

"My hair isn't done," she said, smiling. "What've you got there?"

"A letter—"

"To me?"

I nodded.

"Ah! You want to break off with me," she taunted.

"Madam, didn't you tell me yesterday that I'm not the man for you?"

"*I will repeat it for you, Sir*," she said.

"Very well then." I trembled from head to toe, my voice faltered, I handed her the letter.

"Keep it," she said, eying me coldly. "You forget that it no longer matters whether or not you are satisfactory to me as a *man*. In any case you are good enough as a *slave*."

"Madam!" I cried, indignant.

"Yes, that is how you must address me in the future," replied Wanda, tossing her head with unspeakable contempt. "Arrange your affairs within twenty-four hours. I'm leaving for Italy the day after tomorrow, and you will come along as my servant."

"Wanda—"

"I will brook no familiarity," she cut me off sharply. "Nor will I stand for your entering my quarters without my calling you or my ringing for you, and you will not speak to me unless spoken to. From now on your name is no longer Severin, it is *Gregor*."

I trembled with rage and yet also—I cannot, alas, deny it—with enjoyment and tingling excitement.

"But, Madam, you are acquainted with my circumstances," I began confusedly. "I am still dependent on my father and I doubt whether he will give me the large sum I would need for this journey—"

"In other words, you have no money, Gregor," Wanda remarked in delight. "So much the better. Then you will be completely dependent on me and be truly my slave."

"You fail to consider," I tried to object, "that as a man of honor I cannot possibly—"

"I have indeed considered," she retorted, almost in a tone of command, "that you as a man of honor must above all keep your word, your oath to follow me as a slave wherever I order you and to obey any and all of my commands. Now go, Gregor!"

I turned toward the door.

"Not yet—you may first kiss my hand." She held out her hand with a certain haughty nonchalance, and I—I, a dilettante—I, an ass—I, a wretched slave—pressed her hand with a forceful tenderness to my lips, which were dry with heat and excitement.

A gracious nod. Then I was dismissed.

Late in the evening I still kept a light on and a fire in the large green stove, for I had to put a number of letters and documents in order, and as usual in our area, autumn had broken in with all its might.

Suddenly she tapped the handle of her whip on my window.

I opened the window and saw her standing outside in her ermine-trimmed jacket and a high round Cossack hat of ermine such as Catherine the Great loved to wear.

"Are you ready, Gregor?" she asked grimly.

"Not yet, Mistress," I replied.

"I like that word," she then said. "You may always address me as 'Mistress,' do you understand? We are leaving here tomorrow at nine A.M. Until we reach the district seat you will be my escort, my friend. The instant we board the train you will be my slave, my servant. Now close the window and open the door."

I did as she commanded, and when she came in, she asked, sarcastically knitting her eyebrows, "Well, how do you like me?"

"Wanda—"

"Who permitted you to call me that?" She struck me with the whip.

"You are marvelously beautiful, Mistress—"

Wanda smiled and sat down in the armchair. "Kneel here—here next to my chair."

I obeyed.

"Kiss my hand."

I took hold of her small, cold hand and kissed it.

"And my lips—"

In a surge of passion I flung my arms around the cruel, beautiful woman and covered her face, her lips, her bust with hot kisses, and, shutting her eyes as if in a dream, she responded with the same fire—until past midnight.

At nine A.M. sharp, as she had ordered, everything was ready for the journey. Getting into a comfortable calash, we left the Carpathian resort, where the most interesting drama of my life had woven its plot, its epitasis, and no one could have had an inkling of how it would unravel.

So far, everything was going smoothly. I sat at Wanda's side, and, brimming with charm and wit, she chatted with me, as with a good friend, about Italy, about Pisemsky's[10] new novel and Wagner's music. She was wearing a kind of riding habit, a black cloth frock and a short jacket of the same material with a dark fur trimming; her frock and her jacket adhered snugly to her slender form, emphasizing it marvelously; and she was covered with a dark travel fur. Her hair, knotted in a classical chignon, lay under a small, dark fur hat with a black veil dropping all around. Wanda was in very high spirits, thrusting bonbons into my mouth, playing with my hair, untying my cravat and winding it into a charming little bow, covering my lap with her fur and then stealthily squeezing my fingers. Whenever our Jewish coachman systematically nodded off for a while, she even kissed me, and her cold lips had that fresh, chilly scent of a lone young rose blossoming in autumn amid bare shrubs and yellow leaves, its calyx hung with the small, icy diamonds of the first frost.

Here was the district seat. We got out at the railroad depot. Wanda shed her fur and tossed it over my arm with a charming smile; then she went to buy the tickets.

Upon returning, she was thoroughly transformed.

"Here is your ticket, Gregor," she said in the tone used by arrogant ladies with their lackeys.

"A third-class ticket," I replied with comical dismay.

"Naturally," she went on. "But make sure you don't go to your own car until I'm settled in my compartment and no longer need you. At each stop you are to hurry over and ask for my orders. Do not fail to do so. And now hand me my fur."

After I helped her aboard as humbly as a slave, she looked, followed by me, for a first-class compartment, strode in, leaning on my shoulder, then had me wrap her feet in bearskins and place them on a hot-water bottle.

Next she dismissed me with a nod. I slowly climbed into a third-class car, which was filled with the vilest and densest tobacco smoke the way the fog from the Acheron fills Limbo. And now I had the leisure to meditate on the enigmas of human existence, and on the greatest of these enigmas: *woman*.

Whenever the train halted, I jumped out, dashed to her compartment, and, doffing my cap, awaited her orders. Now she desired a coffee, now a glass of water, at one point a small supper, at another point a basin of warm water to clean her hands. Thus it went. She let herself be courted by a few admirers who had entered her compartment. I was dying of jealousy and had to leap about like a springbok, hurrying to fulfill her demands and get back to my car in time.

Night set in. I could neither eat a morsel nor sleep. I breathed the same oniony air as Polish peasants, Jewish peddlers, and common soldiers, while she, when I mounted the steps to her compartment, lay stretched out on the cushions, in her cozy fur and animal hides—an Oriental despot. And the gentlemen sat upright against the wall, like Indian gods, scarcely daring to breathe.

In Vienna, where she spent one day to do some shopping and, above all, to purchase a set of luxurious garments, she continued treating me as her domestic. I trailed behind her at a respectful distance of ten paces; she handed me her packages without so much as a friendly glance and let me pant along after her, loaded like a donkey.

Prior to our departure, she took all my clothes to donate them to the hotel waiters and ordered me to don her livery: a Cracovian costume in her colors, light blue with red facings and with silver buttons bearing her coat of arms, plus a square red cap adorned with peacock feathers; the outfit didn't suit me all that badly. I felt as if I had been sold or had pledged my soul to the devil.

My beautiful devil took me on a tour from Vienna to Florence. Instead of Mazurs clad in linen and Jews with greasy earlocks, I now had the company of kinky-haired contadini, a magnificent sergeant of the First Italian Grenadiers, and a poor German painter. The tobacco smoke now smelled of cheese and salami instead of onions.

It was night again. I lay on my wooden bed as if on a rack, my arms and legs feeling shattered. Nevertheless the setting had its poetry: The stars were twinkling all around, the sergeant had the face of the Apollo Belvedere, and the German artist crooned a wonderful German song:

> All the shadows darken
> Star upon star sheds light.
> What breath of hot desire
> Flooding through the night!
>
> Through the sea of dreams
> Restlessly my soul,
> Restlessly it steers
> Toward your very soul.

And I thought of the beautiful woman sleeping as calmly as a queen in her soft furs.

Florence! Turmoil, yelling, obtrusive *fachini* and cabmen. Wanda chose a carriage and waved off the porters.

"What do I have a servant for?" she said. "Gregor, here's the ticket—get the luggage."

She wrapped herself in her fur and sat quietly in the carriage while I dragged over the heavy trunks, one after another. For an instant I collapsed under the final one; a friendly carabiniere with an intelligent face came to my rescue. Wanda laughed.

"That one must be heavy," she said, "it contains all my furs."

I clambered up to the driver's seat and wiped the bright drops from my forehead. Wanda gave the cabman the name of the hotel, and he urged the horse on. Within minutes, we fetched up at the dazzling entrance.

"Do you have rooms?" she asked the desk clerk.

"Yes, Madam."

"Two for me, one for my servant, mine with stoves."

"Two elegant rooms for you, Madam, each with a fireplace," replied the *garçon*, hurrying over, "and one without heat for your servant."

"Show me the rooms."

She viewed them, then said curtly, "Fine. I'm satisfied. Just light a fire quickly. My servant can sleep in an unheated room."

I merely looked at her.

"Bring up the baggage, Gregor," she ordered, ignoring my glances. "Meanwhile I'll change and go down to the dining room. You can then have a bite of supper, too."

While she stepped into the next room, I dragged up the trunks and helped the *garçon*—who tried to ask me about my "Mistress" in bad French—to build a fire in her bedroom. With silent envy I momentarily peered at the flaring flames, the white, airy tester bed, the rugs covering the floors. Then, tired and hungry, I went down a stairway and asked for something to eat. A good-natured waiter, who was an Austrian army veteran, made every effort to converse with me in German as he led me to the dining room and served my food. I had just sipped my first drink in thirty-six hours and had my first warm morsel on my fork when she walked in.

I rose.

"How dare you take me to a dining room where my domestic is eating!" she snapped at the garçon, blazing with anger. Then she whirled around and left.

I thanked heaven that I could at least continue eating unimpeded. Next I trudged up the four flights to my room, where my small valise was already standing and a tiny, dirty kerosene lamp was burning. It was a narrow room, with no fireplace, no windows, but with a meager vent hole. If it hadn't been so bitterly cold, it would have reminded me of the *Piombi*, the lead chambers of Venice. I couldn't help bursting into raucous laughter, which echoed so loudly that I was frightened by my own mirth.

Suddenly the door flew open, and the garçon, with a theatrical gesture, truly Italian, called, "You are to go down to Madam at once!" I took my cap, stumbled down a few steps, and at last safely reached the first landing, where I knocked at her door.

"Come in!"

I entered, closed the door, and stood there.

Wanda had made herself at home. Wearing a negligee of white muslin and lace, she sat on a small red velvet couch, her feet on a matching cushion. She wore her fur coat, the one in which she had first appeared to me as the Goddess of Love.

The yellow lights of the candelabra on the pier glass, their reflections in the large mirror, and the red flames in the hearth played marvelously on the green velvet, the dark brown sable of the coat, on her white, smooth, taut skin, and on the red, flaming hair of the beautiful woman. She turned her radiant but icy face toward me and stared at me with her cold green eyes.

"I am satisfied with you, Gregor," she began.

I bowed.

"Come closer."

I obeyed.

"Closer." She looked down and stroked the sable. "Venus in Furs receives her slave. I see that you are no ordinary dreamer. You at least don't lag behind your dreams. You are the sort of man who carries out whatever he imagines, no matter how insane. I must confess I like that, I am impressed. It shows strength, and only strength is respected. I even believe that in unusual circumstances, in an era of greatness, you would reveal your seeming weakness as a wonderful strength. Under the first emperors you would have been a martyr, at the time of the Reformation an Anabaptist, during the French Revolution one of those inspired Girondists who mounted the guillotine with the Marseillaise on their lips. But here you are my slave, my—"

She suddenly leaped up, so that the fur sank down, and she threw her arms around my neck with gentle vehemence.

"My beloved slave, Severin—oh, how I love you, how I worship you, how dapper you look in your Cracovian costume. But you'll freeze up there in your wretched room tonight. Should I give you my fur, my darling, the big fur—?"

She swiftly picked it up, tossed it over my shoulders, and—before I realized what was happening—had wrapped me up in it completely.

"Ah, how beautifully the fur emphasizes your face, it properly brings out your noble features. Once you're no longer my slave, you'll wear a velvet jacket with sable, do you understand? Otherwise I'll never don another fur jacket. . . ."

And she resumed stroking me, kissing me, and finally drew me down to the small velvet couch.

"I think you enjoy wearing this fur," she said. "Hand it over, quick, quick! Otherwise I'll lose all sense of my rank."

I wrapped the fur around her and Wanda slipped her right arm into the sleeve.

"That's what the Titian picture looks like. But enough joking. Don't always have such a morose expression, it saddens me. After all, for now, you're my servant only in the eyes of the world; you're not my slave as yet, you haven't signed the contract as yet. You're still free, you can leave me at any time. You've played your part splendidly. I was delighted. But aren't you fed up already? Don't you find me repulsive? Well, speak—I command you to."

"Must I confess it to you, Wanda?" I began.

"Yes, you must."

"And even if you misuse it," I went on, "I'm more in love with you than ever, and I'll worship you more and more intensely, more and more fanatically the more you mistreat me. The way you've just acted toward me ignites my blood, intoxicates all my senses." I held her tight against me and for several moments clung to her moist lips. "You beautiful woman," I then cried, contemplating her. And in my enthusiasm I tore the sable from her shoulders and pressed my lips on the back of her neck.

"So you love me when I'm cruel," said Wanda. "Go away! You bore me! Don't you hear—?"

She slapped me so hard that I saw stars and my ears rang.

"Help me into my fur, slave."

I helped as best I could.

"How clumsy," she cried; and no sooner did she have the fur on than she slapped my face again. I could feel myself turning white.

"Did I hurt you?" she asked, gently touching me.

"No, no," I cried.

"You mustn't complain, though—you want it this way. Well, give me another kiss."

I wound my arms around her, and her lips clung to mine. As she, in that large, heavy fur, lay on my chest, I had a strange, queasy feeling, as if I were being embraced by a wild beast, a female bear, as if I were about to feel her claws in my flesh. But for this time the bear released me mercifully.

My heart full of joyous hopes, I went up to my wretched servant's room and threw myself down on my hard bed.

"Life is really incredibly funny," I thought to myself. "Moments ago, the most beautiful woman, Venus herself, was resting on your chest, and now you've got the chance to study the hell of the Chinese, who, unlike us, do not fling the damned into flames but let devils drive them out into ice fields.

"The founders of religions must have also slept in unheated rooms."

That night I started from my sleep with a yell. I had been dreaming about an ice field where I had strayed and was futilely trying to escape. Suddenly along came an Eskimo in a sleigh pulled by reindeer; he had the face of the *garçon* who had shown me to the unheated room.

"What are you looking for, Monsieur?" he cried. "This is the North Pole."

A second later he had vanished, and Wanda flew up on small skates across the icy surface, her white satin coat fluttering and rustling. The ermine on her cap and her jacket, and especially her face, were shimmering whiter than the white snow. She shot straight toward me, clasped me in her arms, and began kissing me. Suddenly I felt my warm blood trickling down my side.

"What are you doing?" I cried in dismay.

She laughed, and when I looked at her now, it was no longer Wanda, it was a huge female polar bear drilling her claws into my body.

I screamed desperately and could still hear her diabolical laughter when I awoke and gaped around my room.

Early in the morning I was standing at Wanda's door, and when the *garçon* brought the coffee, I took it and served it to my beautiful Mistress. She was already dressed and she looked marvelous, fresh and rosy; she smiled amiably at me, and called me back when I began respectfully withdrawing.

"Have your breakfast quickly, too, Gregor," she said. "We're going to look at apartments right away. I want to stay in the hotel as briefly as possible. It's terribly awkward here. If I chitchat with you, people instantly say: 'The Russian woman's having an affair with her footman—you can see that Catherine's race is not dying out.' "

Half an hour later, we left the hotel—Wanda in her cloth frock and her Russian cap, I in my Cracovian costume. We caused a sensation. I walked ten paces behind her, frowning, yet fearing that I would burst into raucous laughter at any moment. There was scarcely a street without at least one of the pretty houses flaunting a small sign that announced, "*Camere ammobiliate* (Furnished Rooms)." Each time, Wanda sent me up the stairs, and it was only when I informed her that the place seemed consistent with her requirements that she went up herself. By noon I was as tired as a hound after a hunt.

Again we entered a house and again we left it without finding a suitable apartment. Wanda was in a bad mood. Suddenly she told me, "Severin, your earnestness in playing your role is charming, and the constraint we have put upon ourselves is absolutely thrilling. I can't stand it anymore, you're too darling. I have to kiss you. Come into a house."

"But Madam—" I protested.

"Gregor!" She stepped into the next open vestibule, mounted several steps of a dark staircase, wound her arms around me with ardent tenderness, and kissed me.

"Ah, Severin! You were very smart. As a slave you're more dangerous than I thought. Why, I find you irresistible. I'm afraid I'm going to fall in love with you all over again."

"Don't you love me anymore?" I asked, overcome with sudden dread.

She solemnly shook her head, but kissed me again with her delicious, swelling lips.

We returned to the hotel. Wanda had lunch and ordered me to likewise have a quick bite.

Needless to say, I wasn't served as quickly as she; and so just as I was raising the second morsel of my beefsteak to my mouth, the *garçon* entered and, with a theatrical gesture, called, "To Madam at once."

I took a quick and painful leave of my lunch and, weary and hungry, I dashed over to Wanda, who was already standing in the street.

"I would never, Mistress, have thought you so cruel," I said reproachfully, "as not even to let me eat in peace after all these fatiguing activities."

Wanda laughed heartily. "I assumed you were done," she said, "but never mind. Man is born to suffer, and you especially. The martyrs didn't eat any beefsteaks either."

I followed her, resentful and sullen in my hunger.

"I've given up on the idea of renting an apartment in town," Wanda went on. "It's hard to find an entire floor where one can be secluded and do as one likes. In such a strange and fantastic relationship as ours, everything has to harmonize. I'm going to rent an entire villa and—now, just wait, you'll be amazed. I'm allowing you to eat your fill now and then look around Florence a while. Don't come back before evening. If I need you then, I'll have you summoned."

I viewed the Duomo, the Palazzo Vecchio, the Loggia di Lanzi, and then stood by the Arno for a long time. I gazed again and again at the splendid, ancient city, whose turrets and cupolas were softly delineated in the blue, cloudless sky. I gazed at the splendid bridges, with the beautiful yellow river driving its animated waves through their wide arches. I gazed at the green hills, which, carrying slender cypresses and spacious buildings, palaces or cloisters, surrounded Florence.

We were in a different world, a cheerful, sensual, radiant world. Nor did the landscape have any of the solemnity, the melancholy of ours. Far and wide, to the last white villas scattered in the pale green mountains, there was no spot that the sun did not put in the brightest light. The people were less earnest than we, and might think less, but they all looked happy.

Supposedly, dying is easier in the south.

I now sensed that there are such things as beauty without thorns and sensuality without torment.

Wanda discovered an adorable little villa on one of the charming hills on the left bank of the Arno, across from the Cascine, and she signed a lease for the winter. Located in an attractive garden with delightful lawns, pergolas, and a splendid camellia field, the villa had only two stories and a quadrangular floor plan in the Italian style. One façade was lined with an open gallery, a kind of loggia, with plaster casts of ancient statues and stone steps descending into the garden. From the gallery you reached a bathroom with a magnificent marble basin, from which a spiral staircase led to the Mistress's bedchamber.

Wanda would reside alone on the second floor.

I was assigned a room on the ground floor; it was very pretty and even had a fireplace.

While roaming through the garden, I discovered a small temple on a round hillock. The door was locked, but it had a chink; and when I put my eye to it, I saw the Goddess of Love standing on a white pedestal. I shuddered slightly. She seemed to be smiling at me: "Is that you? I've been expecting you."

It was evening. A petite and pretty maid brought me an order: I was to appear before the Mistress. I climbed the wide marble stairway, crossed the anteroom, a vast, lavishly appointed salon, and tapped on the bedroom door. Intimidated by the ubiquitous luxury, I tapped very softly, and so I wasn't heard and I stood at the door for a while. I felt as if I were standing outside the bedchamber of Catherine the Great, who might emerge at any moment in her green sleeping fur with the red sash on her bare breasts and with her white, powdered little curls.

I tapped again. Wanda impatiently yanked open one wing of the door.

"Why so late?" she asked.

"I was standing at the door, but you didn't hear me knock," I replied shyly. She closed the door behind her, put her arm through mine, and led me to the red damask sofa where she had been resting. All the furnishings in the room—wallpaper, curtains, portieres, canopy bed—everything was in red damask, and the ceiling was covered with a marvelous painting: Samson and Delilah.

Wanda received me in a bewitching dishabille: The satin robe flowed easy and picturesque down her slender body, exposing her arms and bust, which snuggled, soft and yielding, into the dark skins of the large green velvet sable. Her red hair, half undone and held by strings of black pearls, fell down her back to the hips.

"Venus in Furs," I whispered as she drew me to her breasts, threatening to suffocate me with her kisses. I didn't say another word, didn't think another thought; everything drowned in a sea of bliss beyond my wildest dreams.

In the end Wanda gently extricated herself and, propped on one arm, gazed at me. I had sunk down to her feet; she drew me toward herself and played with my hair.

"Do you still love me?" she asked, her eyes blurring in sweet passion.

"How can you ask!" I cried.

"Do you remember your oath?" she went on with a charming smile. "Well, now that everything's set up, everything's prepared, let me ask you again: Are you truly serious about becoming my slave?"

"Am I not your slave already?" I asked in amazement.

"You haven't signed the documents yet."

"Documents? What documents?"

"Ah! I see you've forgotten," she said. "Then let it go."

"But Wanda," I said. "You do know that there's no greater joy for me than to serve you, be your slave. I would give anything to be entirely in your control—I would even give my life—"

"How handsome you are," she whispered, "when you're so enthusiastic, when you talk so passionately. Ah! I'm more in love with you than ever, and now I'm supposed to act domineering toward you and severe and cruel. I'm afraid I won't be able to."

"I'm not worried," I retorted with a smile. "Where are the documents?"

"Here." Half embarrassed, she pulled them from her bosom and gave them to me.

"To make you feel entirely in my control, I've drawn up a second document, in which you state that you are determined to take your own life. I can then kill you if I like."

"Hand it over."

While I unfolded these papers and started reading, Wanda brought pen and ink, then sat with me, put her arm around my neck, and peered at the documents over my shoulder.

The first document said:

Contract between Frau Wanda von Dunajew and Herr Severin von Kusiemski

Herr Severin von Kusiemski ceases as of today to be the fiancé of Frau Wanda von Dunajew and renounces all rights as lover; he then commits himself, on his word of honor as a man and nobleman, to being henceforth the *slave* of Frau von Dunajew until such time as she herself restores his freedom.

As the slave of Frau von Dunajew he is to have the name Gregor, unconditionally fulfill each of her wishes, obey each of her orders, show submissiveness to his Mistress, and view any sign of her favor as an extraordinary grace.

Not only may Frau von Dunajew punish her slave as she sees fit for the slightest oversight or offense, but she also has the right to mistreat him at whim or merely as a pastime, however it happens to please her, and she even has the right to kill him if she so wishes. In short: He is her absolute property.

Should Frau von Dunajew ever grant her slave his freedom, then Herr Severin von Kusiemski must forget everything he has experienced or endured as a slave and *never, under any circumstances whatsoever and in no way, shape, or form whatsoever, consider revenge or retaliation.*

For her part, Frau von Dunajew promises as his Mistress to appear in fur as frequently as possible, especially when she is being cruel to her slave.

Beneath the text, the contract bore the date.

The second document was very brief:

After years of being weary of existence and its delusions, I am, of my own free will, putting an end to my worthless life.

I felt a profound horror when I was done reading. There was still time, I could still back out. But I was swept away by the insanity of passion, the sight of that beautiful woman leaning relaxed on my shoulder.

"First you have to copy this text," said Wanda, pointing to the second document. "It has to be written completely in your hand. Of course, that's not necessary for the contract."

I quickly copied the few lines designating myself a suicide and handed the letter to Wanda. She read it and then, smiling, put it on the table.

"Now do you have the courage to sign this?" she asked, tilting her head with a cunning smile.

I took the pen.

"Let me go first," said Wanda. "Your hand is trembling. Are you so frightened of your happiness?"

She took the contract and the pen. Struggling with myself, I looked up for an instant, and now I was struck by how anachronistic the ceiling painting was, like many paintings of the Italian and Dutch schools. This unhistorical character provided a strange, for me downright sinister, complexion. Delilah, a voluptuous lady with flaming red hair, lay, half undressed, in a dark fur mantle on a red sofa, smiling and bending toward Samson, whom the Philistines had flung down and tied up. In its mocking coquettishness her smile had a truly infernal cruelty; her eyes, half closed, encountered Samson's eyes, which, in their final seeing, still clung to hers with insane love, for one of the foes was already kneeling on Samson's chest, about to blind him with the red-hot poker.

"Goodness," cried Wanda. "You're totally absorbed. What's bothering you? Everything will remain as is even after you sign the agreement. Do you still not know me, darling?"

I looked at the contract. There was her name in large, bold strokes. I peered once again into her magical eyes. Then I took the pen and quickly signed the contract.

"You're trembling," said Wanda calmly. "Should I hold the pen for you?"

That same moment she gently took hold of my hand, and there was my name on the second document. Wanda looked at both documents again and then put them away in the desk that stood at the head of the sofa.

"Fine. Now quickly hand over your passport and your money."

I produced my billfold and handed it to her. She glanced inside it, nodded, and added it to the documents, while I knelt before her, my head resting in sweet intoxication on her bosom.

Suddenly she kicked me away, leaped up, and rang the bell. Three young, slender African women came in—carved out of ebony, as it were, and clad entirely in red satin. Each woman was clutching a rope.

Now I suddenly grasped my situation and I tried to get up. But Wanda, standing erect before me, turning her cold, beautiful, and somber face, her scornful eyes toward me, imperious as my Mistress, gestured. And before I even realized what was happening, the Africans had yanked me to the floor, bound me tightly hand and foot, with my arms behind my back, so that I was like a man about to be executed, barely able to move.

"Give me the whip, Haydée," Wanda ordered with sinister calm.

The African woman knelt and handed the whip to the Mistress.

"And remove this heavy fur from me," Wanda continued. "It's in my way."

The African obeyed.

Wanda then gave another order: "The jacket there!"

Haydée quickly brought the ermine-trimmed kazabaika, which was on the bed, and Wanda slipped into it with two inimitably charming motions.

"Tie him to the column here."

The Africans lifted me up, slung a thick rope around my body, and tied me, standing, to one of the massive columns supporting the canopy of the wide Italian bed.

Then they suddenly vanished as if the earth had swallowed them up.

Wanda hurried over to me, the long train of her white satin gown flowing after her like silver, like moonlight, her hair blazing like flames on the jacket's white fur. She stood before me, her left hand planted on her pelvis, her right hand clutching the whip, and she emitted a brief laugh.

"Now the game-playing has stopped between us," she said, heartlessly cold. "Now the situation is serious, you fool—whom I deride and despise. In your insane blindness, you've surrendered as a plaything to me, an arrogant, capricious woman. You are no longer my lover, you are *my slave*. Your life and your death are at the mercy of my whims.

"You haven't seen anything yet!

"First of all, you will now get a serious taste of the whip—though for no offense on your part—so that you may understand what you can expect if you act clumsy, disobedient, or rebellious."

With savage grace she now hiked up the fur-trimmed sleeve and lashed my back.

I winced—the whip cut into my flesh like a knife.

"Well, how do you like it?" she cried.

I held my tongue.

"Just wait. You'll be whimpering like a dog under my whip," she threatened, and she promptly began to lash me.

The strokes fell quick and dense, with dreadful force, upon my back, my arms, my neck. I gritted my teeth to keep from shrieking. Then she struck my face, warm blood ran down my skin, but she laughed and kept whipping.

"Now I understand you," she cried. "It's really a pleasure to have someone in my power and, in the bargain, a man who loves me—you do love me? No—oh! I'll shred you to bits. My pleasure is growing with every stroke. Writhe a little, scream, whimper! You'll get no mercy from me."

At last she seemed tired.

She tossed away the whip, stretched out on the sofa, and rang.

The African women came in.

"Untie him."

When they loosened the rope, I collapsed on the floor like a chunk of wood.

The black women laughed, baring their white teeth.

"Untie his feet."

They obeyed. I could stand up.

"Come to me, Gregor."

I approached the beautiful woman, who had never looked so seductive as today in her cruelty, in her scorn.

"Another step," Wanda ordered. "Kneel down and kiss my foot."

She stretched her foot out from under the white satin hem, and I, the suprasensual fool, pressed my lips on her foot.

"You will not see me for a whole month, Gregor," she said solemnly, "so that I may become alien to you, and you will adjust more easily to our new relationship. During this time you will work in the garden and await my orders. And now get going, slave!"

A month wore by in humdrum regularity, in hard labor, in mournful yearning, yearning for her, the woman inflicting all this suffering on me. I was assigned to the gardener, helping him to prune trees, clip hedges, transplant flowers, turn over the flowerbeds, sweep the gravel walks, share his crude diet and his hard cot, get up with the chickens and go to bed with the chickens—and from time to time I heard our Mistress enjoying herself, surrounded by admirers, and once I even heard her mischievous laughter all the way down into the garden.

I felt so stupid. Did I become stupid through this present life or had I already been stupid beforehand? The month would be ending the day after tomorrow—what would she do with me now, or had she forgotten me? Would I be trimming hedges and tying bouquets until my dying day?

A written command:

The slave Gregor is hereby ordered into my personal service.

Wanda von Dunajew

With a thumping heart, I parted the damask curtains the next morning and entered my Goddess's bedroom, which was still full of sweet semi-darkness.

"Is that you, Gregor?" she asked while I knelt at the hearth and started a fire. I trembled at the sound of her beloved voice. I couldn't see her, she was resting unapproachably behind the curtains of the canopy bed.

"Yes, Madam," I replied.

"What time?"

"Past nine."

"Breakfast."

I hurried to get it and then, holding the coffee tray, I knelt in front of her bed.

"Here is breakfast, Madam."

Wanda pulled back the curtains and, strangely enough, as I saw her with her undone hair flowing on her white pillows, she at first seemed utterly alien, though a beautiful woman. Those were not the features I loved: that face was hard and had an eerie expression of fatigue, of surfeit.

Or hadn't I had an eye for all that earlier?

She fixed her green eyes on me, more curious than ominous, or somewhat pitying, and she lethargically drew the dark sheepskin over her bared shoulder.

At that moment she was so charming, so bewildering that I felt the blood rushing to my head and my heart, and the tray in my hand began to wobble. She noticed this and reached for the whip that was lying on her night stand.

"You're clumsy, slave," she said, frowning. I lowered my eyes and held the tray as firmly as I could, and she took her breakfast and yawned and stretched her voluptuous limbs in the glorious fur.

She rang. I entered.

"This letter to Prince Corsini."

I hurried into town and delivered the letter to the prince, a young, handsome man with glowing black eyes. Consumed with jealousy, I brought back the response.

"What's wrong?" she asked, with lurking malice. "You're so dreadfully pale."

"Nothing, Mistress, I just walked a bit fast."

At the déjeuner the prince was at her side, and I was condemned to serve both her and him, while they joked, and I didn't exist for either of them. For an instant I blacked out while pouring Bordeaux into his glass: the wine spilled on the tablecloth, on her gown.

"How clumsy," cried Wanda and slapped me. The prince laughed, and she laughed too, and the blood rushed to my face.

After the déjeuner she went off to the Cascine. She herself drove the small carriage with the pretty English chestnuts. I sat behind her and watched her nodding back with a coquettish smile when greeted by any of the august gentlemen.

As I helped her out of the carriage, she leaned lightly on my arm. The contact electrified me. Ah! This woman was truly wonderful, and I loved her more than ever.

A small group of ladies and gentlemen gathered here for dinner at six P.M. I served, and this time I didn't spill any wine on the tablecloth.

A slap is actually more effective than ten lectures. One grasps it so quickly, especially when it is a woman's small, full hand that teaches the lesson.

After dinner she drove to the Teatro della Pergola. Descending the stairs in her black velvet gown with a large ermine collar, a diadem of white roses in her hair, she looked truly dazzling. I opened the carriage door and helped her in. Outside the theater, I leaped from the driver's seat. Stepping out, she leaned on my arm, which quivered under the sweet burden. I opened the door to her box for her and then waited in the corridor. The performance lasted four hours, during which she received visits from her admirers, while I gritted my teeth in anger.

It was far past midnight when the Mistress's bell rang a final time.

"Fire!" she ordered curtly, and when the flames were crackling in the hearth, "Tea."

By the time I returned with the samovar, she had already undressed and was being helped into her white negligee by the African woman Haydée.

Haydée then left.

"Give me the sleeping fur," said Wanda, drowsily stretching her beautiful limbs. I lifted the fur from the easy chair and held it while she slowly and languidly slipped into the sleeves. Then she dropped upon the cushions of the ottoman.

"Take off my shoes and put the velvet slippers on my feet."

I knelt down and tugged on the small shoe, which was resisting me. "Quickly! Quickly!" cried Wanda. "You're hurting me. Just wait—I'll teach you." She lashed me with the whip. I succeeded in doing it right!

"And now march!" A kick—then I was permitted to go to bed.

Tonight I accompanied her to a soiree. In the vestibule she ordered me to help her out of her fur; then with a proud smirk and certain of her victory, she entered the dazzling room. And again hour after hour wore by for me in dismal, monotonous thoughts; from time to time strains of music drifted out to me when the door remained open for an instant. A couple of lackeys tried to converse with me, but since I know only a few words of Italian, they soon gave up.

Eventually I fell asleep and dreamed that I murdered Wanda in a raging fit of jealousy and was condemned to death. I saw myself strapped to the plank, the ax dropped, I felt it in the back of my neck—but I was still alive—

Then the executioner slapped my face.

No, it wasn't the executioner, it was Wanda, standing angrily before me and demanding her fur. I was with her in an instant and helped her into it.

It is really a joy to cloak a beautiful, voluptuous woman in a fur, to see, to feel the back of her neck, her limbs nestling in the soft and exquisite pelt, and to lift her surging curls and place them over the collar. And then, when she tosses off the fur and the sweet warmth and a vague scent of her body cling to the golden tips of the sable hair—it almost drives me insane!

At last a day without guests, without theater, without company. I heaved a sigh of relief. Wanda sat reading in the gallery; she ap-

peared to have no chores for me. At the arrival of twilight and
the silvery evening fog, she withdrew. I served her dinner; she
dined alone, but didn't vouchsafe me so much as a glance, a syl-
lable, or even—a slap.

Ah! How I longed for a slap from her hand.

Tears came to my eyes; I felt how deeply she had degraded
me—so deeply that she didn't even think it worthwhile torturing
me, mistreating me.

Before she went to bed, her bell summoned me.

"You will sleep in my room tonight. Last night I had repulsive
dreams and I'm afraid of being alone. Take a cushion from the
ottoman and lie on the bearskin at my feet."

After snuffing the lights so that only a small lamp hanging
from the ceiling illuminated the room, Wanda got into bed.
"Don't stir, so you won't wake me."

I did as she ordered, but for a long time I couldn't fall asleep.
I saw the beautiful woman, beautiful as a Goddess, lying on her
back in her dark sleeping fur, her arms behind her neck, inun-
dated by her red hair. I heard her magnificent bosom rising in
deep, regular breathing; and whenever she stirred even lightly, I
was awake and listening to see whether she needed me.

But she didn't need me.

I had no other function, no greater significance for her than a
night lamp or a revolver that one places at one's bedside.

Was I crazy, or was she? Did all this stem from an inventive
and mischievous female brain that tried to outdo my suprasensual fantasies? Or did that woman really have one of those
Neronian natures that take a devilish pleasure in controlling people who think and feel and have a will like theirs, in having them
underfoot like a worm?

The things I experienced!

When I knelt before her with the coffee tray, Wanda suddenly
put her hand on my shoulder, and her gaze plunged deep into
mine.

"What beautiful eyes you have," she murmured, "and especially now that you're suffering. Are you terribly unhappy?"

I bowed my head and kept silent.

"Severin! Do you still love me?" she suddenly cried in passion. "Can you still love me?" And she yanked me over so violently that the tray capsized, the cups and the coffeepots fell on the floor, and the coffee ran across the rug.

"Wanda—my Wanda!" I shouted, embracing her violently and covering her lips, her face, her bosom with kisses. "That's my misery—that I keep loving you more and more intensely, more and more insanely the worse you treat me, the more often you betray me! Oh! I'm going to die of pain and love and jealousy."

"But I haven't yet betrayed you, Severin," Wanda countered with a smile.

"No? Wanda! For God's sake! Don't make fun of me so ruthlessly," I cried. "Didn't I personally carry the letter to the prince—?"

"Certainly. A déjeuner invitation."

"Since our arrival in Florence, you've—"

"Remained completely faithful to you," Wanda retorted. "I swear by all that's holy to me. I've done everything purely to make your fantasy come true, purely for your sake.

"But I *will* take on an admirer. Otherwise it's only a halfway measure, and you'll end up reproaching me for not being cruel enough to you. My dear, beautiful slave! Today you're to be Severin again, you're to be only and entirely my lover. I didn't give your clothes away, you'll find them here in the chest. Dress the way you did in the small Carpathian resort, where we loved each other so ardently. Forget everything that's happened since then. Oh, you'll easily forget it in my arms—I'll kiss all your cares away."

She started caressing me, cuddling me, kissing me like a child. Finally, with a sweet smile, she said, "Get dressed now. So will I. Should I wear my fur jacket? Yes, yes, I know. Just get going!"

When I returned, she was standing at the center of the room in her white satin robe and in her red, ermine-trimmed kazabaika; her hair was powdered white, with a small diamond tiara over her forehead. For a moment she reminded me intensely of Catherine the Great. But she left me no time for reminiscing. She drew me down on the ottoman, and we spent two blissful hours. Now she was not the severe, capricious Mistress, she was entirely the fine lady, the affectionate beloved. She showed me photographs, books that had just appeared, and she commented on them with so much intelligence and clarity and good taste and I was so delighted that I brought her hand to my lips more than once. She then had me recite a few poems by Lermontov, and when I got truly enthusiastic, she lovingly placed her little hand on mine and asked, with a sweet expression and a gentle gaze, "Are you happy?"

"Not yet."

She then leaned back in the cushions and slowly opened her kazabaika.

But I swiftly covered her half-exposed breasts with the ermine. "You're driving me insane," I stammered.

"Then come."

I was already lying in her arms, she was already kissing me with a tongue like a snake. Then she again whispered: "Are you happy?"

"Infinitely!" I cried.

She laughed. It was a shrill and nasty laugh that sent shivers up and down my spine.

"Earlier you, the slave, dreamed of being a beautiful woman's toy. Now you imagine you're a free person, a man, my beloved—you fool! A gesture from me and you'll be a slave again. On your knees."

I sank down to her feet, my eyes still clinging skeptically to her eyes.

"You can't believe it," she said, viewing me with her arms crossed on her chest. "I'm bored, and you'll do to while away a few hours. Don't look at me like that."

She kicked me.

"You're simply whatever I want—a person, a thing, an animal." She rang. The African women came in.

"Tie his hands behind his back."

I remained on my knees and put up no resistance. They took me down to the garden, to the small vineyard closing it off toward the south. Corn had been planted in between the vines, and a few dry cobs were still looming here and there. A plow stood off to the side.

The Africans tied me to a post and amused themselves by needling me with their gold hairpins. Before long, however, Wanda came, with the ermine cap on her head and her hands in her jacket pockets. She had the Africans untie me, bind my arms on my back, put a yoke around my neck, and harness me to the plow.

Then her black she-devils pushed me toward the field: One guided the plow, the second led me with a rope, the third drove me along with the whip. And Venus in Furs stood on the side and watched.

When I was serving her dinner the next evening, Wanda said, "Bring me another setting. I want you to dine with me tonight." And when I was about to sit opposite her, she said, "No, sit with me, very close to me."

She was in the best of moods, feeding me soup with her spoon, feeding me morsels with her fork. Then she rested her head on the table like a playful kitten and flirted with me. Haydée was serving the dishes in my stead, and as ill luck would have it, I gazed at her longer than perhaps necessary. I now first observed her noble, almost European features, her splendid, statuesque bust virtually sculpted in black marble. The beautiful she-devil noticed that I was drawn to her and she grinned, baring her teeth. Scarcely had she left the room than Wanda leaped up, blazing with anger.

"What? You dare look at another women in my presence? You must like her better than me—she's more demonic."

I was terrified. I had never seen her like this. Her face and even her lips were suddenly pale and her entire body was trembling. Venus in Furs was jealous of her slave. She tore the whip from its nail and struck me across the face. Next she summoned the black maidservants, and had them tie me up and drag me down to the cellar, where they threw me into a dark, dank subterranean vault—a bona fide dungeon cell.

Then the door slammed shut, was bolted, a key sang in the lock. I was trapped, buried.

I lay there—I don't know how long—trussed up like a calf being hauled to slaughter. I was on a bundle of damp straw, without light, without food, without drink, without sleep. She was perfectly capable of letting me starve to death if I didn't freeze to death first. I was shaking with cold. Or was it fever? I felt myself starting to hate that woman.

A blood-red streak cut across the ground. It was light falling through the opening door.

Wanda appeared on the threshold, wrapped in her sable, and clutching a torch.

"Are you still alive?" she asked.

"Have you come to kill me?" I replied in a dull, hoarse voice.

With two hasty strides Wanda was next to me, kneeling by my pallet, and took my head in her lap. "Are you sick? Your eyes are glowing so intensely. Do you love me? I want you to love me."

She produced a short dagger. I recoiled as its blade flashed before my eyes. I really believed that she was about to kill me. But she laughed and cut the ropes that were binding me.

She would send for me every evening after dinner, have me read to her, and she would discuss all sorts of interesting issues and subjects with me. At such times she seemed like a completely different person. It was as if she were ashamed of the barbarity she had revealed to me, the brutality with which she had treated me. A poignant gentleness transfigured her entire being, and when she held out her hand to me when we said good night, her eyes had that superhuman force of love and goodness that draws our tears, that makes us forget all sufferings of life and terrors of death.

I read *Manon Lescaut* to her. She felt the connection; and though not uttering a word, she smiled from time to time, until she finally closed the small book.

"Don't you wish to read anymore, Madam?"

"Not today. Today we will act out *Manon Lescaut* ourselves. I have a rendezvous in the Cascine, and you, my dear chevalier, will escort me there. I know you'll do it, won't you?"

"You order me."

"I'm not ordering you, I'm asking you," she said with irresistible charm. Then she rose, placed her hands on my shoulders, and gazed at me. "Those eyes!" she cried. "I love you so much, Severin—you have no idea how much I love you."

"Yes," I retorted bitterly. "So much that you're having a rendezvous with another man."

"Goodness, I'm doing that only to provoke you," she replied vivaciously. "I have to have admirers so I won't lose you. I never want to lose you, never, do you hear? I love only you, you alone."

She clung passionately to my lips.

"Oh, if I could only surrender my entire soul to you in a kiss, as I would like to do! But . . . Well, now come."

She slipped into a simple black velvet paletot and enveloped her head in a dark bashlik. Then she walked swiftly through the gallery and mounted the carriage.

"Gregor will drive me," she called to the coachman, who withdrew in astonishment.

I climbed up to the driver's seat and angrily whipped the horses.

In the Cascine, Wanda got out in the area where the main boulevard turns into a bower with dense foliage. It was night; only a few stars were twinkling through the gray clouds drifting across the sky. By the Arno stood a man in a dark coat and a highwayman's hat, gazing at the yellow waves. Wanda hurried through the side bushes and tapped him on the shoulder. I could see him turning to her, taking hold of her hand—then they vanished behind the green wall.

An agonizing hour. At last the leaves rustled off to the side: they were returning.

The man escorted her to the carriage. The lantern light fell full and harsh on a gentle and enraptured face that I had never seen, an infinitely juvenile face surrounded by long blond curls.

She held out her hand, which he so respectfully kissed; then she signaled to me, and instantly the carriage was flying past a long green wall of foliage that screens off the river.

Someone rang at the garden gate. A familiar face. The man from the Cascine.

"Whom shall I announce?" I asked in French. He shook his head, embarrassed.

"Do you understand a little German?" he asked timidly.

"*Jawohl*. I am asking for your name."

"Ah, I don't have one as yet," he answered, abashed. "Just tell your Mistress the German painter from the Cascine is here and would like—but there she is herself."

Wanda stepped out on the balcony and nodded at the stranger.

"Gregor," she called to me, "bring the gentleman up."

I showed the painter to the staircase.

"That's all right, I'll find my way. Thank you, thank you very much." Then he loped up the steps. I remained below, peering after the poor German with deep pity.

Venus in Furs had trapped his soul in the red snares of her hair. He would paint her and lose his mind.

A sunny winter day; the leaves in the clumps of trees and the green grass on the meadow were trembling golden. The camellias at the foot of the gallery shone splendidly in the beautiful wealth of their buds. Wanda sat in the loggia, drawing, while the German painter stood opposite her, folding his hands as if in prayer and watching her—no, he was gazing at her face, utterly absorbed, entranced.

But she didn't see him; nor did she see me clutching a spade, turning over the flowerbeds, merely to see her, feel her presence, which affected me like music, like poetry.

The painter was gone. It was a risk, but I dared. I went up to the gallery, very close, and asked Wanda, "Do you love the painter, Mistress?"

She looked at me without anger, shook her head, and finally even smiled.

"I feel sorry for him," she replied, "but I don't love him. I don't love anyone. *I did love you, as ardently, as passionately, as profoundly as I could love,* but now I don't love you anymore either. My heart is bleak, dead, and that makes me melancholy."

"Wanda!" I cried, painfully moved.

"Soon you'll stop loving me too," she went on. "Tell me as soon as it happens. At that point I'll restore your freedom."

"Then I'll remain your slave all my life, for I worship you and I will always worship you," I cried, seized with that fanaticism of love that had repeatedly been so pernicious for me.

Wanda contemplated me with a bizarre pleasure. "Think about it," she said. "I loved you endlessly and I've been despotic with you in order to make your fantasy come true. Now something of that sweet feeling is still quivering in my breast as ardent sympathy for you. Once this too has vanished, then who knows whether I'll release you? I may become really cruel, ruthless, indeed brutal to you and, while being indifferent or loving someone else, I may take a diabolical pleasure in tormenting, in torturing the man who idolizes and worships me, I may delight in seeing him die of love for me. Think about it!"

"I've long since thought about all this," I replied feverishly. "I can't exist, I can't live without you. I'll die if you give me my freedom. Let me remain your slave—kill me, but don't push me away."

"Well, then be my slave," she answered. "But don't forget that I no longer love you, and so your love has no greater value for me than a dog's—and dogs get kicked."

Today I visited the Medici Venus.

It was still early, the small, octagonal room in the Tribuna was filled with twilight like a sanctuary; and I stood with folded hands, in deep devotion to the mute idol.

But I did not stand for long.

There was no one else in the gallery, not even an Englishman;

and I was already kneeling and gazing at the lovely, slender figure, the budding breasts, the virginal and also voluptuous face
with its half-closed eyes, its foaming curls, which seemed to be
hiding small horns on both sides of the forehead.

The Mistress's bell.

It was noon. But she was still in bed, her arms behind her
neck.

"I'm taking a bath," she said, "and you will attend me. Shut
the door."

I obeyed.

"Now go and make sure the downstairs door is also locked."

I descended the spiral staircase leading from her bedroom
down to the bathroom. My legs buckled, I had to lean on the
iron banister. After making sure the door to the loggia and the
garden was locked, I returned. Wanda now sat on the bed, in her
green velvet fur and with her hair undone. During a swift movement on her part, I saw that she was wearing only the fur, and I
was terrified—I don't know why—as terrified as a condemned
man who knows he is heading toward the scaffold, yet starts to
tremble the moment he sees it.

"Come, Gregor, lift me up."

"Excuse me, Mistress?"

"Well, you are to carry me, don't you understand?"

I lifted her up so that she lay in my arms, while hers were
wound around my neck. And as I slowly descended the staircase
with her, step by step, and her hair struck my cheek every now
and then and her foot lightly braced against my knee, I shook
under the beautiful load and felt that I would have to collapse at
any moment.

The bathroom was a broad and high rotunda, which received
its soft, calm light from the red glass dome overhead. Two palms
spread their huge fronds as a green canopy over a sofa made up
of red velvet cushions, from which steps covered with Turkish
rugs led down to the vast marble basin occupying the center.

"There's a green ribbon upstairs on my nightstand," said

Wanda as I put her down on the sofa. "Bring it and also bring me the whip."

I flew up the staircase and back down and, kneeling, delivered both objects to my Mistress, who then had me tie her heavy, electric hair into a large chignon held together by the green velvet ribbon. Then I drew the bath—and proved quite clumsy, since my hands and legs failed me. The beautiful woman lay on the red velvet cushions, and from time to time I watched her shining now and then amid the dark fur—I couldn't help it, I was compelled by a magnetic force. And whenever I saw her, I felt that all voluptuousness, all lasciviousness is inspired by things that are half concealed, by piquant exposure. And I felt it even more vividly when the basin was full at last, and Wanda threw off her fur coat in a single motion and stood before me like the Goddess in the Tribuna.

At that instant, she looked so chaste, so holy in her uncloaked beauty that I knelt before her as I had knelt before the Goddess, and I pressed my lips devoutly to her foot.

My soul, which, moments ago, had been churned up by such wild waves, all at once flowed calmly, and Wanda likewise displayed no more cruelty toward me.

She slowly descended the steps, and with a silent joy that contained not an atom of torment or yearning, I could watch her dipping up and down in the crystalline liquid, watch the small waves agitated by her and amorously playing around her.

Our nihilistic aesthetician[11] is right: A real apple is more beautiful than a painted one, and a live woman is more beautiful than a Venus of stone.

And when she then emerged from the bath, and the silvery drops and the rosy light trickled down her body—I was overwhelmed by mute ecstasy. I wrapped her in linen cloths, drying her magnificent body; and that quiet bliss lingered with me now, when she, placing her one foot upon me as if on a footstool, rested on the cushions in the large velvet mantle. The supple fur lasciviously snuggled around her cold marble body, and her left arm, on which she propped herself like a slumbering swan, re-

mained in the dark sable of the sleeve, while her right hand care-
lessly played with the whip.

I happened to glance at the massive mirror on the opposite
wall and I cried out, for I saw us in its gold frame as if in a painting; and this painting was so marvelously beautiful, so singular,
so fantastic, that I was grief-stricken to think that its lines, its
colors would dissolve as in a fog.

"What's wrong?" asked Wanda.

I pointed at the mirror.

"Ah! It's really beautiful!" she exclaimed. "Too bad the moment can't be captured forever."

"And why can't it be?" I asked. "Wouldn't every artist, even
the most famous, be proud to immortalize you with his brush if
you allowed him to?

"The mere thought that this extraordinary beauty," I went on,
gazing at her enthusiastically, "this magnificent formation of the
face, these strange eyes with their green fire, this demonic hair,
this splendor of the body is appalling and afflicts me with all the
horrors of death, of annihilation. But the artist's hand should
wrest you from destruction. You must not perish like the rest of
us forever and always, without leaving behind some trace of
your existence. Your picture must live long after you have crum-
bled into dust, your beauty must triumph over death!"

Wanda smiled.

"Too bad modern-day Italy has no Titian or Raphael," she
said. "But perhaps love can make up for genius—who knows?
How about our little German?" She pondered. "Yes—he is to
paint me. And I'll make sure that Cupid blends the pigments."

The young painter set up his studio in her villa—she had trapped
him utterly. He began a Madonna, a Madonna with red hair and
green eyes! He wanted to turn this fiery woman into the image
of virginity: only the idealism of a German can do that. The poor
boy was truly almost a bigger ass than I. Unfortunately our Tita-
nia had discovered our donkey ears *too soon*.

Now she laughed at us, and how she laughed! I could hear her rollicking, melodic laughter in his studio as I stood under the open window, jealously eavesdropping.

"Are you crazy? Me?—Ah! It's incredible—me as the mother of God!" she cried, laughing again. "Just wait! I'll show you a different painting of me—one that I myself painted. You are to copy it for me."

Her face, with her hair flaming in the sunlight, appeared at the window.

"Gregor!"

I dashed up the steps, through the gallery, into the studio.

"Take him to the bathroom," Wanda ordered, hurrying off.

Several moments later, Wanda, dressed only in the sable and clutching the whip, came downstairs and once more stretched out on the velvet cushions. I lay at her feet, and she put one foot on me while her right hand played with the whip. "Look at me," she said, "with your deep, fanatical gaze. Yes—yes, that's it."

The painter had turned abominably pale. He devoured the scene with his lovely, dreamy blue eyes; his lips parted, but he remained mute.

"Well, how do you like the painting?" she asked.

"Yes—that's how I want to paint you," said the German. But that wasn't really speech, that was an eloquent moaning, a weeping of a sick, mortally sick soul.

The charcoal sketch was done, the heads, the flesh tones were filled in, her diabolical face was already emerging in a few bold strokes, her green eyes were flashing with life.

Wanda, her arms crossed on her bosom, stood in front of the canvas.

"Like many paintings of the Venetian school, this should be both a portrait and a narrative," explained the painter, deathly pale again.

"And what do you want to title it?" she asked. "Oh, what's wrong? Are you ill?"

"I'm afraid . . ." he replied, his eyes devouring the beautiful woman in furs. "But let's talk about the painting."

"Yes, let's talk about the painting."

"I imagine the Goddess of Love, who has left Mount Olympus and descended to a mortal man. And since she's always freezing on this modern earth, she tries to warm her sublime body in a huge, heavy fur and her feet in the lap of her beloved. I imagine the favorite of a beautiful female despot, who whips her slave when she is tired of kissing him, and is loved by him all the more insanely the more she kicks him. And so I will call the painting: *Venus in Furs*."

The painter painted slowly. But his passion grew all the faster. I was afraid that he would ultimately take his own life. She was playing with him, providing enigmas, and he couldn't solve them and he felt his blood tingling—but she was amused.

While sitting for him, she nibbled on bonbons, made tiny balls from the paper wrappers and pelted him with them.

"I'm delighted that you're in such high spirits, Madam," said the painter, "but your face has completely lost the expression I need for my painting."

"The expression you need for your painting," she echoed, smiling. "Please be patient for just one moment."

She pulled herself up and lashed me with the whip. The painter gaped at her, flabbergasted, with a childlike mixture of repugnance and admiration.

As she whipped me, Wanda's face took on more and more of that cruel, scornful character that so dreadfully delights me.

"Is this the expression you need for your painting?" she called. The confused painter lowered his eyes before the cold beam of her gaze.

"That's the expression . . ." he stammered. "But now I can't do anything. . . ."

"What?" said Wanda mockingly. "Could I perhaps help you?"

"Yes," cried the painter, virtually insane. "Whip me too."

"Oh! With pleasure," she replied, shrugging. "But if I'm to whip, I want to whip in earnest."

"Whip me to death," cried the painter.

"Will you let me tie you up?" she asked, smiling.

"Yes . . ." he moaned.

Wanda left the room for a moment and returned with ropes.

"Well—do you still have the courage to surrender uncondi-tionally to Venus in Furs, the beautiful despot?" she began deri-sively.

"Tie me up," replied the painter in a sullen voice. Wanda bound his hands behind his back, drew one rope through his arms, a second one around his body, and secured him to the crossbars of the window. Then she rolled up her fur sleeves, took hold of the whip, and stepped before him.

For me the scene had a ghastly charm that I cannot depict. I felt my heart pounding as she laughed and hauled back for the first blow, and the whip whistled through the air, and the painter winced slightly; and then, with her red lips parted, her teeth flashing between them, she tore away at him until his poignant blue eyes seemed to beg for mercy—it was indescribable.

She sat alone for him now. He was working on her head.

She posted me behind the heavy door curtain, where I was unseen but saw everything.

What was on her mind?

Was she afraid of him? She had driven him insane enough—or was it to be a new torture for me? My knees trembled.

They were talking. His voice was so soft that I couldn't catch anything, and she answered in an equally soft voice. What did that mean? Were they conniving?

I was suffering dreadfully, my heart was ready to burst.

Now he knelt before her, he embraced her and pressed his head into her bosom—and she, the cruel woman, she laughed—and now I heard her loudly exclaiming:

"Ah! You need the whip again."

"Woman! Goddess! Have you no heart? Are you unable to love?" cried the German. "Don't you even know what it means to love, to be devoured by yearning, by passion? Can't you even imagine what I'm suffering? Don't you have any pity for me?"

"No!" she replied, haughty and mocking. "But I do have the whip." She swiftly pulled it from the pocket of her fur and struck his face with the shaft. He stood up and retreated several steps.

"Can you paint again now?" she asked, indifferent. Instead of answering, he returned to the easel and picked up his brush and his palette.

The painting was marvelous; it was a portrait, an incomparable likeness, and it also seemed to depict an ideal, for the colors were so intense, so miraculous, so diabolical I might say.

The painter had simply painted all his torment, his adoration, his malediction into the painting.

Now he painted me; we spent several hours daily alone. One day he suddenly turned to me with a quivering voice: "You love this woman?"

"Yes."

"I love her too." His eyes were bathed in tears. He held his tongue for a while and kept painting.

"In Germany there's a mountain where she lives," he then murmured to himself. "She's a devil!"

The painting was completed. She wanted to pay him for it, the way queens pay.

"Oh, you've already paid me!" he said, begging off with a painful smile.

Before leaving he secretly opened his portfolio to let me peer inside. I was dumbfounded. Her face stared at me, virtually alive, as if from a mirror.

"I'm taking this along," he said. "It's mine. She can't snatch this, I worked hard enough for it."

"I really do feel sorry for the poor painter," she said to me. "It's silly to be as virtuous as I am. Don't you think?"

I didn't dare answer her.

"Oh, I forgot I was talking to a slave. I have to go out, I need diversion, I want to forget. Quick! My carriage!"

A new, fantastic attire: Russian ankle-boots of violet, ermine-trimmed velvet; a gown of the same material, decorated with narrow stripes and gathered up with cockades of the identical fur; a short, close-fitting paletot similarly lined and padded with ermine; a high ermine cap à la Catherine the Great, with a small osprey fastened with a diamond agrafe; her undone red hair flowing down her back. She climbed to the driver's seat and drove the carriage herself; I sat behind her. How she whipped the horses! The team raced along in a frenzy.

She apparently wanted to create a sensation today and she fully succeeded. Today she was the lioness of the Cascine. People in carriages greeted her; groups formed on the footpath, talking about her. But she paid no heed to anyone, though now and then she nodded slightly to acknowledge a greeting from an elderly cavalier.

Suddenly a young man came galloping along on a wild and slender black horse. The instant he saw Wanda, he reined in and walked his mount—he was already very close, he halted, and watched her ride by. And now she spotted him—the lioness the lion. Their eyes met—and as she raced past him, she was unable to tear herself away from the magical force of his gaze, and her head turned back.

My heart stood still at this half-marveling, half-delighted gaze with which she devoured him; but he deserved it.

He *was* a handsome man, by God. No, more: he was a man such as I had never seen in the flesh. He stands in the Belvedere, hewn in marble, with the same slender and yet iron muscles, the same face, the same rippling curls. And what actually made him so peculiarly beautiful was that he wore no beard; and had his pelvis been less narrow, he might have been mistaken for a woman in male disguise . . . and that strange line around his mouth, the leonine lips that revealed a bit of the teeth and momentarily gave the face a touch of cruelty—

Apollo flaying Marsyas.

He sported high black boots, snug breeches of white leather, a short fur jacket like the kind worn by Italian cavalry officers, of black cloth with an astrakhan trimming and a rich frog; and on his black curls a red fez.

Now I understood male Eros and admired Socrates for re-
maining virtuous with Alcibiades.

I had never seen my lioness so excited. Her cheeks were still
blazing when she sprang from the carriage at the perron outside
her villa. As she hurried up the steps, she imperiously motioned
me to follow.

Striding to and fro in her room, she began speaking with a
haste that terrified me:

"You will find out who that man in the Cascine was—today,
immediately—

"Oh, what a man! Did you see him? What do you think? Say
something!"

"The man is handsome," I answered sullenly.

"He's so beautiful. . . ." She paused and leaned on the back of
a chair. "He took my breath away."

"I can understand the impact he made on you," I replied. My
imagination again recklessly whirled me away. "I was beside myself, and I can picture—"

"You can picture," she laughed, "this man as my lover, whipping you and you enjoying the whipping.

"Go now, go."

By evening, I had tracked him down.

Wanda was still fully dressed when I returned; she lay on the
ottoman, her face buried in her hands, her hair tangled like a
lion's red mane.

"What's his name?" she asked, unbelievably calm.

"Alexis Papadopolis."

"So he's Greek."

I nodded.

"Is he very young?"

"Barely older than you. They say he was educated in Paris
and they call him an atheist. He fought against the Turks in Can-
dia and supposedly distinguished himself no less through his
racial hatred and his cruelty than through his bravery."

"So all in all, a man," she cried with sparkling eyes.

"At present he lives in Florence," I went on. "Supposedly he's incredibly rich—"

"I didn't ask about that," she cut in swiftly and sharply. "That man is dangerous. Aren't you afraid of him? I'm afraid of him. Does he have a wife?"

"No."

"A mistress."

"No again."

"Which theater does he attend?"

"Tonight he'll be at the Teatro Nicolini, where the brilliant Virginia Marini and Salvini are performing. Salvini is Italy's, perhaps Europe's, premier living actor."

"Get me a box there—quick, quick!" she ordered.

"But Mistress—"

"Do you want to taste the whip?"

"You can wait down in the lobby," she said after I placed her opera glass and her program on the balustrade of her box and adjusted the footstool.

Now I stood there and had to lean against the wall to keep from collapsing with envy and fury—no, fury wasn't the right word. It was mortal dread.

I could see her in her box, in her blue moiré gown, with the large ermine mantle around her bare shoulders, and him across from her. I could see them devouring one another with their eyes, I could see that for them the stage, Goldoni's Pamela, Salvini, Marini, the audience, indeed, the world had gone under—and I: what was I at that moment?

Tonight she attended the ball at the Greek ambassador's home. Did she know she would run into that man there?

At least she dressed as if she would. A heavy aquamarine silk gown adhered sculpturally to her divine curves, leaving her arms and her throat bare; in her hair, which formed a single flaming chignon, she wore a blossoming water lily, from which green

reeds, interwoven with a few loose braids, fell down the back
of her neck. No trace of her excitement, of her trembling fever-
ishness: she was calm, so calm that my blood froze, and I felt
my heart turning cold under her gaze. Slowly, with weary and
indolent majesty, she ascended the marble stairs, let her costly
wrap glide down, and nonchalantly entered the ballroom, which
the smoke from a hundred candles had filled with a silvery
mist.

For several moments I peered after her, forlorn; then I picked
up her fur, which, without my realizing it, had slipped from my
hands. It was still warm from her shoulders.

I kissed the warmth, and tears flooded my eyes.

There he was.

In his black velvet jacket, which was lavishly trimmed with
dark sable: a beautiful, arrogant despot, toying with human lives
and human souls. He stood in the antechamber, looked around
haughtily, and fixed his eyes on me for an uncomfortably long
time.

Under his icy stare I was again seized with that dreadful mortal terror, an inkling that this man could capture her, fascinate
her, subjugate her; and I felt inadequate next to his savage virility,
I felt envious, jealous.

How deeply I felt my identity as the feeble and eccentric man
of intellect! And the most shameful thing of all: I wanted to hate
him but couldn't. And how had he managed to ferret me out in
the swarm of domestics?

With an inimitable grandiose nod, he signaled me to come
over, and I . . . I followed that signal—against my will.

"Remove my fur," he calmly ordered.

My entire body shook with indignation, but I obeyed, as ab-
ject as a slave.

I spent the entire night in the antechamber, delirious as in a fever. Bizarre images drifted past my mind's eye: I could see them
meeting—that first long gaze. I could see her floating through

the ballroom in his arms, intoxicated, her head lying on his chest with half-closed eyes. I could see him in the sanctuary of love, not as a slave but as a master, reclining on the ottoman with her at his feet; I could see myself serving him on bended knees, the tea tray wobbling in my hands, and I could see him reaching for the whip. Now the servants were talking about him.

He was a man like a woman. He knew he was beautiful and behaved accordingly; he would change his coquettish attire four or five times a day, like a vain courtesan.

In Paris he had appeared first in women's garb, and the men had stormed him with love letters. An Italian singer, famous equally for both his art and his passion, invaded the Greek's apartment, knelt down, and threatened to take his own life if his plea was not granted.

"I am sorry," the Greek responded with a smile. "It would be my pleasure to fulfill your request, but you have no other choice than to carry out your death sentence, for I am—a man."

The crowd had significantly thinned out—but she apparently had no intention whatsoever of leaving.

Morning was already seeping through the blinds.

Finally I heard the rustle of her heavy gown, which flowed behind her like a green wake: she came, step by step, conversing with him.

I now scarcely existed for her; she didn't even bother giving me an order.

"Madame's coat," he commanded. Naturally he never even dreamed of attending to her himself.

While I helped her into the fur, he stood next to her with crossed arms. But when I, kneeling, put the fur shoes on her feet, she lightly leaned her hand on his shoulder and asked:

"What was that about the lioness?"

"When the lion whom she has chosen, with whom she lives, is attacked by another," said the Greek, "the lioness calmly reclines and watches the battle. And if her mate is defeated, she does not help him—she indifferently looks on as he perishes in his own blood under his opponent's claws, and she follows the victor, the stronger lion. Such is a woman's nature."

At that instant my lioness shot me a strange glance. I shuddered—I didn't know why; and the early red light dipped me and her and him in blood.

She didn't go to bed. She merely tossed off her ball garments and undid her hair. Then she ordered me to start a fire, and she sat by the hearth and stared into the glowing flames.

"Do you need me anymore, Mistress?" I asked, my voice faltering at that last word.

Wanda shook her head.

I left the room, walked through the gallery, and sat down on the steps leading into the garden. From the Arno a light northerly wind wafted fresh, moist coolness; the green hills, both near and distant, stood in rosy fog; golden haze floated about the city, about the cupola of the Duomo.

A few stars were still quivering in the pale blue sky.

I tore open my jacket and pressed my hot forehead against the marble. Everything that had occurred so far seemed like child's play; but now the situation was serious, horribly serious.

I sensed catastrophe: I saw it before me, I could hold it in my hands; but I lacked the courage to face it, my strength was broken. And to be honest: it wasn't the pains I dreaded, or the sufferings that could sweep over me, or the abuse that might lie in store for me.

What I felt was fear—a fear of losing the woman whom I loved almost fanatically; and this fear was so violent, so crushing that I suddenly burst out sobbing like a child.

All day long she remained locked in her room, waited on by the African woman. When the evening star first glowed in the blue ether, I saw her walk through the garden and, cautiously trailing her at a distance, I saw her enter the Temple of Venus. I stole after her and peered through the chink in the door.

She stood before the sublime effigy of the Goddess, her hands folded as if in prayer, and the sacred light of the star of love cast its blue rays upon her.

In my bed at night, my fear of losing her, my despair grabbed hold of me with a violence that made me a hero, a libertine. In the corridor I lit the small red oil lamp suspended under the image of a saint and, cupping the light with one hand, I stepped into her bedchamber.

The lioness, driven to exhaustion, hunted to death, had at last fallen asleep on her cushions; she lay on her back, clenching her fists and breathing heavily. She seemed to be frightened by a dream. Slowly I withdrew my hand from the lamp and let its full red light fall upon her wonderful face.

But she did not wake up.

I gently set the lamp on the floor, sank down by Wanda's bed, and put my head on her soft, hot arm.

She stirred for an instant, but again she did not wake up. I don't know how long I lay there, in the middle of the night, turned to stone by ghastly tortures.

Eventually I was seized with a violent spasm and I was able to weep—my tears flowed over her arm. She winced several times. Finally she sat up, startled, rubbed her eyes, and looked at me.

"Severin," she cried, more frightened than angry.

I found no answer.

"Severin," she went on softly. "What's wrong? Are you sick?"

Her voice was so sympathetic, so kind, so loving that it seared into my chest with red-hot tongs, and I began sobbing loudly.

"Severin!" she started anew. "You poor, unhappy friend." Her hand gently stroked my curls. "I feel sorry, very sorry for you. But I can't help you—for the life of me I don't know of any remedy for you."

"Oh, Wanda! Does it have to be?" I moaned in my pain.

"What, Severin? What are you talking about?"

"Don't you love me at all anymore?" I went on. "Don't you feel even a little pity for me? Has the handsome stranger already taken you over completely?"

"I can't lie," she gently countered after a brief pause. "He did have an effect on me that I can't grasp, that makes me suffer and tremble. It's the kind of impact that I've found described by poets, that I've seen on stage—but I've always regarded it as a figment of the imagination. Oh! That man is like a lion, strong and beautiful and proud, and yet soft, not brutal like our men in the north. I do feel sorry for you, believe me, Severin. But I must possess him—what am I saying? I must surrender to him if he wants me."

"Think of your reputation, Wanda—you've always preserved it so immaculately," I cried, "even if I no longer mean anything to you."

"I *am* thinking of it," she replied. "I want to be staunch for as long as I can, I want—" Ashamed, she buried her face in the cushions. "I want to be his wife—if he wants me."

"Wanda!" I shouted, again seized with that mortal fear that robbed me each time of breath, of reason. "You want to be his wife, you want to belong to him forever! Oh, don't push me away! He doesn't love you—"

"Who says so?" she cried, flaring up.

"He doesn't love you," I continued passionately. "But I do love you, I worship you, I'm your slave. I want to be trampled by you, I want to carry you in my arms through life."

"Who says he doesn't love me?" she vehemently broke in.

"Oh, be mine!" I pleaded. "Be mine! I can't exist, I can't live without you. Have pity, Wanda, pity!"

She looked at me, and now she again had that same cold, heartless gaze, that malicious smirk.

"You say he doesn't love me," she said mockingly. "Well, fine, console yourself with that." She rolled over, contemptuously showing me her back.

"My God, aren't you a woman of flesh and blood? Don't you have a heart as I do?" I cried, my chest heaving convulsively.

"You know what I am," she retorted nastily. "I'm a woman of stone, *Venus in Furs*, your ideal—just kneel and worship me."

"Wanda!" I pleaded. "Mercy!"

She burst out laughing. I pressed my face into her cushions and wept a stream of tears in which my pain dissolved.

There was a long silence; then Wanda slowly sat up.

"You bore me," she began.

"Wanda!"

"I'm sleepy, let me sleep."

"Mercy," I pleaded. "Don't push me away. No other man, no one else will love you as I do."

"Let me sleep. . . ." She turned her back to me.

I sprang up, reached for the dagger hanging next to her bed, yanked it from its sheath, and put it to my chest. "I'll kill myself here before your very eyes," I murmured sullenly.

"Do as you like," replied Wanda, utterly indifferent. "But let me sleep."

Then she yawned loudly. "I'm very sleepy."

For an instant I stood there, turned to stone; then I began to laugh and again weep loudly. Finally I thrust the dagger in my belt and fell to my knees before her.

"Wanda—please listen to me for just a few seconds," I begged.

"I want to sleep! Can't you hear?" she screamed angrily, leaping from her bed and kicking me away. "Have you forgotten that I'm your Mistress?" And when I still didn't budge, she grabbed the whip and lashed me. I got to my feet. She hit me again—this time in the face.

"Damn it, slave!"

Holding a clenched fist aloft and suddenly resolute, I left her bedroom. She tossed the whip away and broke into loud laughter—and I can imagine I was quite comical in my theatrical posture.

I was determined to tear myself away from the heartless woman, who had treated me so cruelly and was now about to betray me faithlessly in the bargain—as a reward for my slavish worship, for everything I had endured from her. So I packed my few belongings in a kerchief and wrote her a letter:

Madam,

I loved you insanely, I surrendered to you as no man has ever surrendered to a woman. But you have abused my most sacred emotions and played an impudent, frivolous game with me. So long as you were merely cruel and pitiless, I could still love you; but now you are about to turn common. *I am no longer the slave who lets you kick him and whip him. You yourself have freed me, and I am leaving a woman whom I can only hate and* despise.

Severin von Kusiemski

I handed this note to the Moorish female and then hurried away as fast as I could. By the time I reached the train station, I was out of breath. I felt a violent pang in my heart—I halted . . . I burst into tears. Oh! It was shameful—I wanted to flee and couldn't. I would turn back—where? To her—whom I both reviled and worshiped.

Again I changed my mind. I couldn't go back. I mustn't go back.

But how could I leave Florence? I realized I had no money, not a penny. Well, then on foot. Begging honestly is better than eating a courtesan's bread.

Yet I couldn't leave.

She had my pledge, my word of honor. I had to go back. Perhaps she would release me from my promise.

After several quick steps, I halted again.

She had my word of honor, my oath, that I was her slave so long as she wanted, so long as she herself didn't grant me freedom. But I *could* kill myself after all.

I walked through the Cascine down to the Arno, all the way down, where its yellow water, splashing monotonously, washed a few forlorn willows. There I sat and settled my account with existence—my whole life passed before me, and I found it quite wretched: a few joys, an infinite number of worthless and indifferent things, interspersed with richly sown pains, sufferings, anxieties, disappointments, shattered hopes, grief, sorrow, and ruefulness.

I thought of my mother, whom I loved so much and whom I had seen dying slowly of a dreadful illness; I thought of my brother, who, with all his claims to pleasure and happiness, had died in the prime of his youth without even having set his lips to the beaker of life. I thought of my dead wet nurse, my childhood playmates; I thought of my friends, who had striven and studied with me—all those who were covered by the cold, dead, indifferent earth. I thought of my turtledove, who had not infrequently cooed and bowed to me instead of to his mate—all dust to dust returned.

I laughed loudly and slid into the water—but at that same moment I grabbed a willow branch dangling over the yellow waves. And I saw the woman who had made me miserable: she was floating above the watery surface, the sun shining through her as if she were transparent, with red flames around her head and neck. She turned her face toward me and smirked.

I was back again, soaked, dripping, burning with shame and fever. The African woman had delivered my note; so I was judged, doomed, in the hands of a heartless, offended woman.

Well, let her kill me! I—I couldn't do it. Yet I didn't want to go on living.

As I walked around the house, she stood in the gallery, leaning on the balustrade, her face in the full sunlight, blinking at me with her green eyes.

"Are you still alive?" she asked without stirring. I stood there stupidly bowing my head.

"Give me back my dagger," she went on. "You have no use for it. Why, you don't even have the courage to end your own life."

"I don't have the dagger," I replied, trembling, shaken by cold.

She sized me up with a proud, contemptuous glance.

"You must have lost it in the Arno." She shrugged. "Who cares? Well, and why haven't you left?"

I muttered something that neither she nor I could make out.

"Oh, you have no money!" she cried. "Here!" And she tossed her purse at me with an unspeakably disdainful gesture.

I didn't pick it up.

We both remained silent for a very long time.

"So you don't want to leave?"

"I can't."

Wanda drove to the Cascine without me, she went to the theater without me; when she entertained, the African woman did the serving. No one asked about me. I wandered restlessly through the garden like an animal that's lost its master.

Lying in the bushes, I watched a pair of sparrows fighting over a seed.

Then I heard the rustle of a woman's garment.

Wanda was approaching in a dark silk frock that was modestly buttoned up to her throat. The Greek was with her. They were engaged in a lively conversation, but I didn't catch a single word. Now he stamped his foot so hard that the gravel flew apart, and he lashed the air with his riding crop. Wanda recoiled.

Was she afraid he'd strike her?

Had they gone that far?

He left her, she called him, he didn't hear, he didn't want to hear.

She nodded sadly, then settled on the nearest stone bench; she stayed there for a long time, lost in thought. I watched her with something like gleeful joy. At last, I vehemently pulled myself together and scornfully went over to her. She was startled and she trembled from head to foot.

"I've come to congratulate you," I said, bowing. "I see, dear Madam, that you have found your Master."

"Yes, thank goodness!" she cried. "No new slave—I've had enough slaves. A Master. A woman needs a Master and she worships him."

"So you worship him, Wanda!" I shouted. "That brutal man—"

"I love him more than I've ever loved anyone else."

"Wanda!" I clenched my fists, but tears were already coming to my eyes, and a frenzy of passion seized me—a sweet insanity. "Fine, then choose him, marry him. Let him be your Master, but I will remain your slave for as long as I live."

"You'd be my slave even then?" she said. "That would be piquant. But I'm afraid he won't put up with it."

"He?"

"Yes, he's already jealous of you," she cried. "He of you! He's demanded that I dismiss you on the spot. And when I told him who you are—"

"You told him . . ." I repeated, frozen.

"I told him everything," she replied. "I told him our entire story, all your strange desires, everything. And he, instead of laughing, he lost his temper and stamped his foot."

"And threatened to hit you?"

Wanda looked down in silence.

"Yes, yes!" I said, scornfully bitter. "You're afraid of him, Wanda!" I fell to her feet and, agitated as I was, I embraced her knees. "I want nothing from you, nothing but to remain near you forever—your slave! I want to be your dog!"

"Do you realize you're boring me?" said Wanda apathetically.

I sprang up. Everything in me was boiling.

"Now you're no longer cruel, now you're common!" I said, stressing every word sharply and pungently.

"You already said so in your letter," Wanda countered with a haughty shrug. "An intelligent man should never repeat himself."

"The way you treat me!" I erupted. "What do you call that?"

"I could discipline you," she retorted scornfully, "but this time I prefer to respond with explanations rather than lashes. You have no right to accuse me of anything. Haven't I always been honest with you? Haven't I warned you more than once? Didn't I love you deeply, even passionately, and did I hide the fact that it is dangerous to surrender to me, to grovel in front of me—did I hide the fact that I want to be dominated? But you wanted to be my plaything, my slave! You found supreme joy in feeling the foot, the whip of a cruel and arrogant woman. So what do you expect now?

"Dangerous tendencies lay dormant in me, and you were the first to arouse them. If I now take pleasure in torturing you, mistreating you, then it's all your fault. You turned me into what I am now, and you're actually unmanly and weak and miserable enough to blame it on *me*."

"Yes, it's my fault," I said. "But haven't I suffered for it? Put an end to it now! Stop this cruel game!"

"I want to end it too," she replied with a strange, devious look.

"Wanda!" I cried vehemently. "Don't make me go to extremes. You can see that I'm a man again."

"A flash in the pan," she countered. "A flame that crackles for an instant and goes out just as quickly as it blazed up. You think you can intimidate me, but you're merely ridiculous. If you had been the man I originally thought you were—earnest, pensive, rigorous—I would have loved you faithfully and become your wife. A woman desires a man she can look up to. But if a man— as you have done—voluntarily offers her his neck for her foot, then she will use him as a welcome toy and fling him away when she's tired of him."

"Just try to fling me away," I said scornfully. "Some toys are dangerous."

"Don't challenge me," cried Wanda, her eyes sparkling, her cheeks flushed.

"If I can't have you," I went on, choking with anger, "then no one else can have you either."

"What play are you quoting?" she mocked. Then she grabbed my chest; she was utterly pale with anger. "Don't challenge me," she continued. "I'm not cruel, but I myself don't know how far I can go or whether there would be any limit."

"What can you do to me that's worse than making him your lover, your husband?" I replied, blazing hotter and hotter.

"I can make you his slave," she threw back. "Aren't you in my control? Don't I have the contract? But of course, it will only be a pleasure for you if I have you tied up and I tell him: 'Do whatever you like to him.' "

"Woman, are you crazy?!" I shrieked.

"I'm very sane," she said calmly, "I'm warning you for the last time. Don't try to resist me. Now that I've gone this far I can easily go further. I feel something like hatred for you. I would truly enjoy watching him whip you to death, but I'm still holding back, still . . ."

Almost out of my mind, I grabbed her wrist and pulled her to the ground, so that she was kneeling before me.

"Severin!" she cried, her face twisting in rage and terror.

"If you become his wife, I'll kill you!" I threatened. The words came hoarse and dull from my chest. "You're mine, I won't let you, I love you too much." I clutched her and held her tight, and my right hand automatically reached for the dagger in my belt.

Wanda fixed her large, calm, incomprehensible eyes on me.

"You appeal to me like this," she said coolly. "Now you're a man, and I know at this moment that I still love you."

"Wanda." My ecstasy brought tears to my eyes. I leaned over her and covered her enchanting little face with kisses, and she, suddenly bursting into loud, spiteful laughter, cried, "Have you had enough of your ideal now? Are you satisfied with me?"

"What?" I stammered. "You haven't been serious."

"I *am* serious," she gaily went on, "about loving you, you alone. And you, you good little fool—didn't you notice that everything was just a game, just make-believe? Didn't you notice how hard it often was for me to whip you, when I would really have preferred to take your face in my hands and cover it with kisses? But we've had enough, haven't we? I played my cruel role better than you expected. Now you must be satisfied to have your good, smart, and not unattractive little wife—aren't you? We have to live in a sensible way and—"

"You'll be my wife!" I cried, exulting with bliss.

"Yes—your wife, you dear, sweet man," whispered Wanda, kissing my hands.

I drew her up to me.

"So! Now you're no longer Gregor, my slave," she said. "Now you're my darling Severin again, my husband."

"What about him? You don't love him?" I asked, agitated.

"How could you possibly believe that I love that brutal man—but you were completely blinded—I was worried about you. . . ."

"I almost killed myself because of you."

"Really?" she cried. "Ah, I still tremble at the thought that you were already in the Arno. . . ."

"But you saved me," I replied tenderly. "You floated above the water and smiled, and your smile called me back to life."

It was a strange sensation now holding her in my arms, with her resting mutely on my chest, letting me kiss her and smiling. I felt as if I had suddenly awoken from a feverish delirium or as if I had been shipwrecked and had spent several days fighting with the waves that threatened to swallow me up at any moment—and now I had finally been cast ashore.

"I hate Florence—you've been so unhappy here!" she exclaimed when I said good night. "I want to leave immediately, tomorrow. Please write a few letters for me, and while you're busy with that, I'll drive to town and make my farewell visits. Is that all right with you?"

"Of course, my dear, good, sweet wife."

Early in the morning she knocked at my door and inquired how I had slept. Her kindness was truly delightful. I would never have thought that she could be so gentle.

She had been gone for over four hours. Having long since finished my letters, I sat in the gallery, peering at the road and trying to spot her carriage in the distance. I was a little anxious about her, and yet goodness knows I had no reason to doubt or fear. But my distress lurked in my heart, and I couldn't get rid of it. Perhaps it was the sufferings of days past that still threw their shadow on my soul.

There she was, radiant with happiness, contentment.

"Well, has everything gone as you wished?" I asked her, tenderly kissing her hand.

"Yes, my darling," she replied, "and we're leaving tonight. Help me pack my bags."

Toward evening she asked me go to the post office and drop off her letters. I took her carriage and was back in an hour.

"The Mistress asked about you," said the African woman, smiling, as I went up the broad marble staircase.

"Has someone been here?"

"No one," she answered, crouching on the steps like a black cat.

I walked slowly across the hall and now stood at the door to Wanda's bedroom.

Why was my heart pounding? I was so happy, after all.

Slowly opening the door, I pushed back the portiere. Wanda lay on the ottoman; she seemed not to notice me. How beautiful she was in her silver-gray silk frock, which clung so revealingly to her splendid figure, exposing her wonderful bust and her arms. Her hair was bound up and twisted through with a black velvet ribbon. A roaring fire was blazing in the hearth, the ceiling lamp was shedding its red light—the entire room was swimming in blood.

"Wanda!" I finally said.

"Oh, Severin!" she cried joyfully. "I've been waiting for you so impatiently." She leaped up and enclosed me in her arms; then she sat back down in the sumptuous cushions and tried to draw me to her. But I gently glided down to her feet and put my head in her lap.

"Do you know that I'm very much in love with you today?" she whispered, brushing some stray hair from my forehead and kissing my eyes.

"How beautiful your eyes are. That's what I've always liked most about you. But today they're absolutely intoxicating. I'm dying. . . ." She stretched out her marvelous limbs and tenderly blinked at me through her red eyelashes.

"And you—you're cold. You're holding me like a chunk of wood. Just wait—I'll make you love me!" she cried, again caressing, cuddling, clinging to my lips.

"You don't like me anymore—I have to be cruel to you again. I'm obviously too nice to you today. Do you know what, little fool? I'm going to whip you again. . . ."

"But my darling—"

"I want to."

"Wanda!"

"Come, let me tie you up," she continued, hurrying wickedly around the room. "I want to see you truly in love, do you understand? Here are the ropes. Can I still do it?"

First she tied my feet, then she bound my hands tightly behind my back and finally pinioned my arms as if I were a criminal.

"So," she said cheerfully. "Can you still move?"

"No."

"Good. . . ."

She then made a noose from a strong rope, tossed it around my head, and lowered it to my hips. Then she drew it tight and attached me to a bedpost.

At that moment I was seized with a strange tremor.

"I feel as if I'm being executed," I murmured.

"Well, you're going to be thoroughly whipped again today!" cried Wanda.

"But wear your fur jacket," I said. "Please."

"I can give you that pleasure," she replied, getting her kazabaika and putting it on with a smile. Then she stood with her arms crossed on her bosom and peered at me through half-closed eyes.

"Do you know the story of the bull of Dionysius?" she asked.

"I remember it very vaguely. What about it?"

"A courtier dreamed up a new torture instrument for the tyrant of Syracuse—an iron bull, in which a condemned man was to be locked and placed over a huge fire. As soon as the iron bull began to glow and the victim screamed, his wailing would sound like the bellowing of a bull.

"Dionysius smiled graciously at the inventor and, in order to test his work on the spot, he ordered him to be the first to be shut in the iron bull.

"The story is very instructive.

"It was you who inoculated me with selfishness, arrogance, and cruelty, and *you are to be their first victim*. Now I actually find pleasure in capturing a man who thinks and feels and desires, as I do—a man who is stronger than I in mind and body. I find pleasure in controlling him, mistreating him—especially a man who loves me.

"Do you still love me?"

"Insanely!" I cried.

"All the better," she answered. "You will then derive all the more enjoyment from what I am now going to do to you."

"What's wrong with you?" I asked. "I don't understand you. Today your eyes are really flashing with something like cruelty, and you're so strangely beautiful—so entirely *Venus in Furs*."

In lieu of replying, Wanda put her arms around my neck and kissed me. At that instant I was again overwhelmed by the full fanaticism of my passion.

"Well, where is the whip?" I asked.

Wanda laughed and took two steps back.

"So you absolutely want to get whipped?" she cried, haughtily tossing her head.

"Yes."

All at once, Wanda's face was utterly transformed, as if twisted with anger. For a moment she even looked ugly.

"Then whip him!" she cried loudly.

That same instant the beautiful Greek thrust his head with its black curls through the curtains of her canopy bed. At first I was speechless, numb. The situation was dreadfully funny—I would have laughed myself if it hadn't been so desperately dismal, so degrading for me.

It surpassed my fantasies. Cold shivers ran up and down my spine as my rival stepped forth in his riding boots, his snug white breeches, his short velvet jacket, and my eyes fell on his athletic physique.

"You are truly cruel," he said, turning to Wanda.

"Only a pleasure-seeker," she retorted with wild humor. "Pleasure alone makes existence worthwhile. A pleasure-seeker has a difficult time parting from life. The person who is needy or suffers welcomes death like a friend. But the person who wants pleasure has to take life cheerfully as people did in ancient Greece. He mustn't shy away from indulging at other people's expense, he must never feel pity. He must harness others to his carriage, to his plow like animals. He must enslave people who feel, who wish to have pleasure like him; he must exploit them without regret for his service, for his delights. He must never ask whether they feel good about it or whether they perish. He must always bear in mind: If they had me in their control, they would do the same to me, and I would have to pay for their enjoyments with my sweat, my blood, my soul. Such was the world of the Ancients. Enjoyment and cruelty, freedom and slavery have always gone hand in hand. People who want to live like Olympian gods must have slaves whom they throw into their fishponds and gladiators who fight during their masters' sumptuous banquets—and the pleasure-seekers never care if some blood splatters on them."

Her words brought me fully to my senses.

"Untie me!" I yelled angrily.

"Aren't you my slave, my property?" replied Wanda. "Should I show you the contract?"

"Untie me!" I threatened loudly. "Or else—" I strained at the ropes.

"Can he get loose?" she asked. "He threatened to kill me."

"Don't worry," said the Greek, testing my bonds.

"I'll scream for help," I began again.

"No one will hear you," countered Wanda, "and no one will prevent me from again abusing your most sacred feelings and playing a frivolous game with you." And with satanic scorn she repeated the phrases of my letter.

"Do you find me merely cruel and ruthless at this moment or am I about to get *common*? What? Do you still love me or do you already hate and despise me? Here is the whip." She handed it to the Greek, who hurried over to me.

"Don't you dare!" I cried, shaking with outrage. "I won't put up with anything from you—"

"You believe that only because I'm not wearing fur," the Greek retorted with a frivolous smirk, and he took his short sable from the bed.

"You're delicious!" cried Wanda, kissing him and helping him into the fur.

"May I really whip him?" he asked.

"Do whatever you like to him," replied Wanda.

"Beast!" I sputtered indignantly.

The Greek fixed his cold tigerish glare on me and tested the whip. His muscles swelled as he hauled back and let it whistle through the air; and I was bound like Marsyas and had to watch Apollo preparing to flay me.

My eyes wandered about the room and paused on the ceiling, where Samson, at Delilah's feet, was being blinded by the Philistines. At that moment the painting struck me as a symbol, an eternal allegory of man's passion, lust, his love for woman. "Each of us is ultimately a Samson," I thought to myself, "and, like it or not, we are ultimately betrayed by the woman we love, whether she wears a cloth bodice or a sable fur."

"Now observe me training him," cried the Greek. He bared his teeth, and his face took on the bloodthirsty expression that had frightened me the very first time I had seen him.

And he began to whip me—so ruthlessly, so dreadfully, that I winced under every stroke, and my entire body began trembling in pain. Indeed tears ran down my cheeks, while Wanda lay on the sofa, clad in her fur jacket and propped on one arm, watching with cruel curiosity and convulsed with laughter.

There is no describing the feeling of being mistreated by a successful rival in front of the woman you worship. I was dying of shame and despair.

And the most humiliating thing of all was that in my woeful situation, under Apollo's whip and amid the cruel laughter of my Venus, I initially felt a kind of fantastic, suprasensual fascination—but Apollo lashed the poetry out of me, stroke by stroke, until I finally clenched my teeth in powerless rage and cursed myself, my lustful imagination, cursed women and love.

I suddenly saw with dreadful clarity how blind lust and passion have led men since Holofernes and Agamemnon into the snare, into the net of the treacherous woman, into misery, slavery, and death.

It was like awakening from a dream.

My blood was already flowing under the whip, I was writhing like a worm being trampled; but he kept pitilessly whipping away, and she kept pitilessly laughing away while closing the packed trunks, slipping into her traveling fur—and she was still laughing as she strode down the stairs on his arm and mounted into the carriage.

Then everything was silent for an instant.

I listened breathlessly.

Now the carriage door shut, the horses started trotting, the carriage rolled for a while—then everything was over.

For an instant I thought of taking revenge, killing him; but I was bound by the wretched contract. I had no choice but to keep my word and clench my teeth.

My first desire after that cruel catastrophe of my life was to find strenuous tasks, danger, deprivation. I wanted to join the army and go to Asia or Algiers; but my father, who was old and ill, needed me.

So I quietly returned home and for two years I helped him endure his troubles and run the estate; and I learned something that I hadn't previously known and that now revived me like a drink of fresh water: *to work and to fulfill obligations*. Then my father died, and I became the landowner; but nothing else changed. I put on the Spanish boots and I now lead a fairly reasonable life as if the old man were standing behind me, peering over my shoulder with his large, intelligent eyes.

One day I received a crate accompanied by a letter. I recognized Wanda's handwriting.

Strangely moved, I opened the letter and read:

Mein Herr,

Now that three years have flowed by since that night in Florence, I must again confess to you that I loved you very deeply. But you yourself smothered my feelings with your fantastic surrender, with your insane passion. The moment you became my slave, I felt that you could never be my husband; but I found it piquant to embody your ideal and perhaps, while having delicious fun, to cure you.

I found the strong man whom I needed and with whom I was as happy as one can be on this comical ball of clay.

But, like all human happiness, mine was very brief. Roughly a year ago he was killed in a duel, and I have been living in Paris ever since, like an Aspasia.

And what about you? Your life can't possibly lack sunshine if your imagination has lost its hold on you, and those features that at first drew me so powerfully have come to the fore in you: clarity of thought, kindness of heart, and, above all: moral earnestness.

I hope that you were healed under my whip; the therapy was cruel but radical. To remind you of that time and the woman who passionately loved you, I am sending you the portrait painted by the poor German.

Venus in Furs

I had to smile, and as I became absorbed in my thoughts, the beautiful woman in the ermine-trimmed velvet jacket suddenly stood before me, whip in hand. And I continued smiling at the woman I had loved so insanely, at the fur jacket that had once delighted me so deeply, at the whip. And I finally smiled at my pains and I said to myself: "The therapy was cruel but radical. The main thing is: I am healed."

"Well, and the moral of the story?" I asked Severin, placing the manuscript on the table.

"The moral is that I was an ass," he cried without turning toward me—he seemed embarrassed. "If only I had whipped her."

"A curious method," I replied. "It may work with your peasant girls—"

"Oh, they're used to it," he answered briskly. "Imagine the effect, however, on our fine, high-strung, hysterical ladies. . . ."

"But what about the moral?" I asked.

"The moral is that woman, as Nature has created her and as she is currently reared by man, is his enemy and can be only his slave or his despot, *but never his companion*. She will be able to become his companion only when she has the same rights as he, when she is his equal in education and work.

"Now we have the choice of being either hammer or anvil, and I was an ass to make myself a woman's slave—do you understand? Hence the moral of the story: He who lets himself be whipped deserves to be whipped.

"The blows, as you see, were highly beneficial. The rosy, suprasensual fog has dissolved, and no one will make me again believe that the sacred monkeys of Benares or Plato's rooster are the image of God."[12]

APPENDIX

TWO CONTRACTS SIGNED BY SACHER-MASOCH

(Contract between Frau Fanny von Pistor and Leopold von Sacher-Masoch.)

Herr Leopold von Sacher-Masoch agrees on his word of honor to be the slave of Frau von Pistor and unconditionally fulfill her every wish and every order for a period of six months.

For her part, Frau von Pistor cannot demand anything dishonorable of him—anything that would make him disreputable as a human being and a citizen. Furthermore she must leave him six hours daily for his work and never look at his letters or writings. At every offense or negligence or lèse-majesté, the Mistress (Fanny Pistor) may punish her slave (Leopold von Sacher-Masoch) as she sees fit and at her own discretion. In short, her subject, Gregor, must display slavish submission to his Mistress, take any bestowal of her favor as a delightful gift, and make no demand on her love or assert any right as her lover. Fanny Pistor, in return, promises to wear fur as often as practical and especially when being cruel.

After a period of six months, this slavery intermezzo is to be regarded by both sides as having never happened, and no serious allusion is to be made to it. Everything is to be viewed as forgotten, and both sides are to return to their earlier amorous relationship. [Later deleted.]

These six months need not be in direct sequence; they can be interrupted for long periods of time and end and start according to the Mistress's whim.

This contract is confirmed by the signatures of the partici-
pants.

Taking effect on 8 December 1869

Fanny Pistor Baddanow
Sir Leopold von Sacher-Masoch

(Contract between Sacher-Masoch
and Wanda von Dunajew.)

My slave!

The conditions under which I accept you as my slave and tolerate you at my side are as follows:

Completely unconditional surrender of your self.

You have no will outside of me.

You are a blind tool in my hands, following *all* my orders
without contradiction. Should you forget that you are my slave
and should you fail to show me unconditional obedience in all
matters, I have the right to punish and chastise you *entirely at
my own discretion,* and you are not to so much as dare complain
about it.

Anything pleasant or felicitous that I grant you is to be regarded as a *favor* and must be gratefully taken by you only *as
such;* I have no *obligation,* no *indebtedness* toward you.

You may not be my *son, brother,* or *friend,* you are nothing
but my slave lying in the dust.

Just like your body, *your soul* also belongs to me, and if that
makes you suffer, you must nevertheless subjugate your feelings,
your emotions to my domination.

I am permitted to exercise the *greatest cruelty,* and even if I
maim you, you are to endure it without complaint. You must labor for me like a slave, and if I revel in luxury while keeping you
deprived and kicking you, you must unprotestingly kiss the foot
that has kicked you.

I can dismiss you *at any moment,* but you must never be away
from me without my permission; and should you flee from me,

you grant me the power and the right *to torture you to death with any conceivable torments*.

Aside from me you have nothing, I am everything to you: your life, your happiness, your unhappiness, your torment, and your pleasure.

You must carry out anything I demand, *good* or *evil*, and if I demand a crime from you, then you must become a *criminal* in obedience to my will.

Your honor belongs to me as do your blood, your mind, your capacity for work; I am your Mistress over life and death.

If ever you can no longer bear my domination, and the chains become too heavy for you, then you must kill *yourself*—I will *never* give you your freedom.

I commit myself on my word of honor to be the slave of Frau Wanda von Dunajew, in exact accordance with her demands, and to submit unresistingly to everything that she imposes on me.

Dr. Leopold Knight von Sacher-Masoch

EXPLANATORY NOTES

1. Staff: According to legend, Tannhäuser, trying to repent for his sensual life in the service of Frau Venus, was told by Pope Urban that his sins could not be forgiven any more than the staff in his hand could blossom. But three days later the staff began sprouting green leaves. Unfortunately, Tannhäuser had disappeared forever.
2. Hegel: We can't really fault the narrator for dozing off while reading Hegel—even though the passage was probably from "Master and Servant" in *The Phenomenology of Mind.*
3. Galicia was the Austrian name for a large multiethnic province of the Habsburg monarchy, including Poles, Jews, Germans, and Ruthenians or Ukrainians. Galicia was created from the partitioned lands of the Polish-Lithuanian Commonwealth in the late eighteenth century, became part of Poland again after World War I, and is today divided between Poland and Ukraine. The administrative capital of the Habsburg province was called Lwów in Polish, Lemberg in Germany, Lemberik in Yiddish, and Lviv in Ukrainian.
4. *Manon Lescaut* (1731), a novel penned by Antoine François Prévost, a Benedictine monk, describes the obsessive love that the Chevalier des Grieux develops for Manon, thereby causing his own doom. The story was treated in operas by Massenet and Puccini.
5. Creator: the Greek legend of the sculptor Pygmalion, whose beautiful statue of a woman came to life.
6. Circe in the *Odyssey.*
7. Aspasia: the most famous of the Ionian courtesans and the mistress of the Greek historian Pericles.
8. Astarte, the Semitic goddess of love and nature, was eventually identified with Aphrodite/Venus in Greco-Roman mythology.
9. Peter Schlemihl, the man who sold his shadow to the devil, figures in stories by German writers Adalbert Chamisso and Hoffmann as well as in Offenbach's opera *The Tales of Hoffmann.* His name derives from the Yiddish word for "unlucky person."
10. Aleksey Feofilaktovich Pisemsky (1820–1881) was a Russian realist

125

author. His best works describe the life of the common people, whom he got to know intimately when investigating conditions in the Russian interior.

11. The "nihilistic aesthetician" is presumably Nietzsche.

12. The "sacred monkeys of Benares" was one of Schopenhauer's ways of describing women.

Plato's rooster: Diogenes snatched up a rooster, tossed it into Plato's school, and exclaimed: "This is Plato's human being."

In every corner of the world, on every subject under the sun, Penguin represents quality and variety – the very best in publishing today.

For complete information about books available from Penguin – including Puffins, Penguin Classics and Arkana – and how to order them, write to us at the appropriate address below. Please note that for copyright reasons the selection of books varies from country to country.

In the United States: Please write to Penguin USA Inc., 375 Hudson Street, New York, New York 10014.

In the United Kingdom: Please write to Dept JC, Penguin Books Ltd, FREEPOST, West Drayton, Middlesex UB7 0BR.

In Canada: Please write to Penguin Books Canada Ltd, 10 Alcorn Avenue, Suite 300, Toronto, Ontario M4V 3B2.

In Australia: Please write to Penguin Books Australia Ltd, P.O. Box 257, Ringwood, Victoria 3134.

In New Zealand: Please write to Penguin Books (NZ) Ltd, Private Bag 102902, Auckland 10.

In India: Please write to Penguin Books India Pvt Ltd, 706 Eros Apartments, 56 Nehru Place, New Delhi 110 019.

In the Netherlands: Please write to Penguin Books Netherlands bv, Postbus 3507, NL-1001 AH Amsterdam.

In Germany: Please write to Penguin Books Deutschland GmbH, Metzlerstrasse 26, 60594 Frankfurt am Main.

In Spain: Please write to Penguin Books S.A., Bravo Murillo 19, 1º B, 28015 Madrid.

In Italy: Please write to Penguin Italia s.r.l., Via Felice Casati 20, I-20124 Milano.

In France: Please write to Penguin France S.A., 17 rue Lejeune, F-31000 Toulouse.

In Japan: Please write to Penguin Books Japan, Ishikiribashi Building, 2-5-4, Suido, Bunkyo-ku, Tokyo 112.

In South Africa: Please write to Longman Penguin Southern Africa (Pty) Ltd, Private Bag X08, Bertsham 2013.